BOY BAND

Jacqueline E. Smith

Wind Trail Publishing

BOY BAND

Wind Trail Publishing
PO Box 830851
Richardson, TX 75083-0851
www.WindTrailPublishing.com

Second Paperback Edition, May 2019

ISBN-13: 978-0-9896734-4-0
ISBN-10: 0-9896-7344-8

Cover Photo: Katherine June
Cover Design: Wind Trail Publishing

This is a work of fiction. Characters, places, and incidents portrayed in
this novel are either products of the author's imagination or used
fictitiously.

For everyone who knows what it is to appreciate good music…
Especially boy bands. And for my sister.

Chapter One

"I hate to see you down
You know a face so beautiful
Should never bear a frown
Now I don't know what time will bring
Could be waiting here a while
But girl I have to tell you
The world's a little brighter
When you smile..."

Song: "Brighter"
Artist: The Kind of September
From the Album: *17 Times Over*

"Okay Mel, I've got one. Would you rather eat bugs for the rest of your life or endure the zombie apocalypse with no personal hygiene products whatsoever?"

It's weird being in love with your best friend. If you've never experienced it, let me lay it out for you.

He's the guy you grew up with. The one who used to pull your hair and chase you around the playground. The one who would spend hours playing "time travel adventure" in the secret clubhouse you constructed beneath the dining room table. He even gave you your first kiss when you were ten, but now that you're older, you both pretend it didn't happen because if you acknowledge it, then things might get awkward.

He's the guy that evolved from that weird, hyper kid who wasn't allowed to eat sugar to the tall, cool, hilarious guy that everyone loves. He has big blue eyes and thick, messy dark blond hair that falls literally everywhere and a smile that could probably knock someone out.

He's the guy you didn't want to fall in love with because you know that if he ever figured it out, things might not ever be the same between you, and you love the way things are. You love that he still teases you and confides in you. You love that you're his best friend too, and that nothing feels more natural than being with him.

It was impossible to not fall in love with him, and yet, a part of you still curses the day you did, because in all the years you've been friends, you've never had a reason to lie to him.

But for the most part, you love that you love him, because when you go to sleep at night, you actually look forward to waking up in the morning because you know you'll get to see him. You could be having the worst day imaginable, and just a few words from him will make it tolerable, even enjoyable. You don't love him because he's cute or funny or because being close to him makes you weak at the knees.

You love him because he's *him*.

"Sam, have you noticed that all your 'Would You Rather' questions end up going back to the zombie apocalypse?" I ask.

"That's because zombies are awesome," Sam insists, shoveling popcorn into his mouth.

"No they're not. Zombies can kill you."

"You still haven't answered the question," he reminds me.

"Eating bugs or unhygienic zombies." Both are lousy options. "Well, I'm pretty much dead either way since I'd starve to death in the first scenario, and I wouldn't last long enough in the zombie apocalypse to get all that dirty... So I guess I'll go with eating bugs."

2

"Really?"

"Yeah. At least there are no zombies."

I'm pretty sure all friends play "Would You Rather," but for the longest time, Sam was convinced he'd invented it. Like, he was absolutely adamant that no one else in the entire universe had ever sat around and asked each other if they would rather be caught sniffing their fingers or picking their nose. Somehow, we never ask each other positive things, like if we would rather have perfect hair for the rest of our lives or own our own private island. It's always something miserable, gross, or potentially embarrassing. Usually a combination of the three.

"Okay, fine. Your turn."

It's sort of hard to come up with good questions that I don't already know the answer to, but I give it a go nevertheless. "Okay, would you rather watch nothing but chick flicks for the rest of your life or be confined to a room made completely out of sponge?"

"Eugh. Chick flicks. No question."

Sam has this really weird sponge phobia. Apparently it's a real thing. He gets super grossed out by the idea of sponges, or anything porous, really. He just hates things with a lot of little holes. Empty corn cobs freak him out too. Like, he loves eating corn on the cob, but the minute he's done with it, he can't get it off his plate quick enough. Last summer in Australia, he and the guys went scuba diving on the Great Barrier Reef. I told him, somewhat jokingly, to watch out for sponge coral, and I swear to you, he almost didn't go. Fortunately for the rest of us, he didn't see any. We would have been hearing about it for the rest of the trip.

"That one was too easy," I grumble.

"You know me better." He grins before tossing a handful of popcorn my way. I try to dodge it, but a few pieces still bounce off my head and onto my laptop. I've been trying to get some work done for the last two hours, but I think it goes without saying that having Sam around is a bit distracting.

"Ew, now my keyboard is all buttery," I pretend to complain.

"Want me to lick it off?" Sadly, he's not flirting. He's just being gross.

"Not if your tongue's been where all the tabloids say it's been," I remark.

"Oh yeah? Who am I dating this week?"

"Last time I checked, it was Kelli Barnett, but she may have dumped you already."

"Yeah, she wishes she could have that honor."

Kelli Barnett is probably the world's most annoying D-list celebrity. I truly have no idea why she's famous. To be honest, I don't think anyone really does. All I know is that she was on some really bad televised contest a few years back and now has her own reality show. It's the kind of show that everyone loves to hate because all it really shows is Kelli and her equally irritating posse stirring up stupid and unnecessary drama. Last year, she dated this basketball player, cheated on him with one of his teammates, and then tried to sue the first guy after the story broke. The idea that Sam would even consider dating her is, quite frankly, a little hilarious.

Then again, he's not dating me, so maybe I shouldn't be laughing.

"Alright, it's my turn. Would you rather – "

But before he can get the words out, the door to the lounge opens and Joni appears, looking less frazzled than usual, but still a little on the edge.

"Sam, there you are. I've been looking everywhere for you. Come on, you're supposed to be in makeup by now."

"Mel's fault. She was distracting me," he claims. I can only hope we never end up in any sort of serious trouble. He'd sell me out in a heartbeat.

"Not interested. You're a big boy now. You should be able to keep an eye on the time all by yourself," Joni scolds him as she escorts him out the door. Before she leaves, she turns back to me. "Are you going to watch the interview, Mel?"

"I'll be there in a minute. I just have to finish up this assignment." Most of the time, I enjoy my online college courses. Other times, I have to admit, they can be a bit of a drag.

"Okay, but just remember, the guys go on at 2, but I'm pretty sure they won't be letting people in or even backstage after 1:30. Just so you know."

"Thanks, Joni," I tell her. She leaves, shutting the door behind her.

1:30. That gives me 45 minutes until I have to be down in the studio to watch the guys on *The Happening Now Show with Jim and Kacy*. They're going to be debuting their new single, "This Is Real." The Internet has been buzzing about it for days.

Like I said, it's weird being in love with your best friend.

It's even weirder when the rest of the world is in love with him, too.

The Kind of September is one of the planet's most popular bands. They have two albums out, both platinum, and they're about to release their third, which, like the first two, will probably soar right to the top of the charts. The band members include Josh Cahill, Cory Foreman, Oliver Berkley, Jesse Scott, and the one and only Sam Morneau.

Josh is your stereotypical funny guy. He loves pulling pranks, telling jokes, and just making people laugh in general. He's zany and hyper and I'm pretty sure if he ever got his hands on an energy drink, the world might actually implode. But he's also one of the most genuine people I know. He's super sweet, always has time for fans, loves dogs probably more than anyone else in the known universe, and has a mild obsession with Spiderman. Girls go crazy not only for his cute personality, but his big brown eyes and stylish blond hair.

Cory is the one who everyone sees as a big brother. Then again, maybe that's just me. I've been friends with Cory and his twin sister, Joni, almost as long as I've been friends with Sam. But you know, I really don't think it's just me. Cory is really tall, with green eyes and long dark hair that's always made me think of a Muppet. He's also very protective of everyone he loves. He's probably the most conscientious and responsible member of the group. For example, he's the only one without a tattoo and he's the only one who's ever actually on time to anything.

Oliver is - there is no other way to put it - very British. He and his family moved here while we were all still in high school and all of us girls were instantly smitten. It's the same way for him now that he's famous, but now, instead of a few schoolgirls with a crush, it's the entire female population of Earth. He's not very tall, but he has big brown eyes, curly brown hair, and probably the best smile of all the guys in the group. He's very polite and owns more wool sweater vests than anyone I've ever met. And yes, he wears them. All the time.

Then there's Jesse. Jesse is the sexy, rocker bad boy. Or at least, he's supposed to be. He might look the part - tall and built, with stylish auburn hair and light blue eyes - but he's neither a rocker nor a bad boy. He's not even a little broody. He's actually really smart, writes a ton of the guys' music, and he started up his own charity for homeless animals. Even though he'll never admit it, he has a huge heart and I've actually seen him tear up over sad puppies and kittens. Jesse is really kind of a dreamboat. Though technically, I'm not supposed to think that.

See, Jesse and Joni used to date. They were really cute in high school. They went to Homecoming together and everything. But once the band got big, things kind of fell apart between them. I'm not sure if Joni got jealous of all the attention that he was suddenly receiving or if Jesse wanted a little freedom to go with his newfound fame. Either way, he broke up with her, and the split wasn't exactly what you'd call amicable. They're still civil to one another. They kind of have to be since Joni works with them and her brother is one of his bandmates. But I know there's still some resentment there, at least on Joni's side.

Finally, there's Sam. Wild, crazy, adorable Sam. The guy of everybody's dreams. He's not the best singer in the group. He's not even the best looking. But he's everyone's favorite. It might have something to do with his bad jokes or his smile or maybe his charisma. Whatever the reason, everyone loves Sam Morneau.

Including me.

"Welcome back to *The Happening Now Show*! Our next guests are international pop megastars who have won millions of hearts all across the globe. They rose to fame two years ago with the release of their self-titled debut album, and their second, *17 Times Over*. Now, they're preparing for the release of their third album, *Meet Me on the Midway*. Ladies and gentlemen, please welcome The Kind of September!"

The crowd (mostly girls) goes absolutely wild before Kacy finishes her introduction. It gets even louder when the guys actually appear on stage. By now, I'm sure they're used to it, but in the beginning, the constant screams and tears and declarations of love used to freak them out. It was actually kind of cute. Now, they're still cute, but they're calm and confident and have been instructed on how to smile and wave at the fans, which is just what they do as all five take a seat on Jim and Kacy's famous purple couch.

"Welcome, guys! Good to have you on the show!" Kacy greets them.

"Thanks! It's great to be here!" Cory replies, acting as the group's formal spokesperson.

"I have to tell you my nieces are huge fans. They love you so much that they both started crying when I told them you were going to be on the show."

"Aw. Well, tell them that we say hello!" Sam grins.

"We'll get them some autographs after the show. I'm sure it will be no problem," Oliver offers.

"That would officially make me the favorite aunt ever," Kacy exclaims.

"So clearly, you guys are pretty popular with the ladies," Jim comments.

Again, the girls in the audience scream. The guys look pretty bashful. Well, four of them do. Jesse just kind of smirks and relishes it. He was used to girls falling over him even before he was famous. Girls fell all over Sam too, but back then, he just sort of laughed it off. When I asked him why, he said it embarrassed him. I'm not sure if it still does, but he definitely still blushes any time someone calls him cute or dreamy.

"Are there any special ladies in your lives?" Jim continues. "Sam, I know we've been seeing a lot of you in the gossip columns."

"Yeah, I don't really read those," he answers.

"Oh really? Why not?"

"They sort of scare me."

The audience responds with a chorus of laughter and more than a few rounds of,

"Aww..."

"They scare you?" Kacy asks.

"Yeah! I don't want to know what people think I'm doing. Most of it is really weird. If everything on the Internet about me was true... I don't know, I think I'd actually be dead now."

He's right. Last year, a rumor circulated on Twitter that all the guys except for Josh had been killed in a fiery car crash. Who starts these rumors and why, I'll never know. Thankfully, I was with them when I heard about their supposed demise, so I got to avoid the meltdown that would have followed had I really believed that they were gone.

"Fair enough," Kacy laughs. "So, how about the rest of you? Any special ladies?"

"Josh's mom is pretty nice," Jesse jokes. The crowd laughs again.

"I have a girlfriend now," Cory admits.

A few girls sigh, but most suppress cries of anguish. Next to me, Joni scowls and crosses her arms. She's not particularly fond of Cory's new girlfriend, an aspiring model named Tara Meeks. I don't really feel like I know her well enough to judge one way or the other, but Joni is convinced that Tara is "only dating Cory in order to utilize his fame and publicity for personal gain and social advancement." Her words, not mine. I'm not that articulate.

But Cory is totally into Tara. And why not? She's tall (much taller than I'll ever be), slender, and drop-dead gorgeous. Of course she's gorgeous. She's a model. She has thick blonde hair, big amber eyes, and whenever she's around, I swear Cory's IQ drops about sixty points. She's *that* beautiful.

The problem is that's all I really know about her. Well, that and she's really into tweeting about their relationship.

@ItsTaraMeeks: Just had best date ever with my boo, #CoryForeman of #TKOS #LoveHimSoMuch #PopStar

@ItsTaraMeeks: New earrings from #CoryForeman! He spoils me rotten! #LoveOfMyLife #TKOS

@ItsTaraMeeks: Don't you just love it when your dreamy boyfriend sings to you? #CoryForeman #Celebrity #TKOS

Maybe Joni has a point. But I'm still willing to give Tara the benefit of the doubt. Cory is a great guy and I think he's smart enough to know a good girl when he meets one. At least, I hope he is. I'm afraid I'm still a bit naive when it comes to relationships, especially in this crazy world of fame and fortune.

By now, the interview is over and Kacy and Jim are in the middle of announcing, " - the world debut of The Kind of September's newest single from their new album available next month, ladies and gentlemen, 'This is Real.'"

As always, the guys line up with their handheld microphones. I know they're really excited to share this song. They've been working on it forever, and they're really proud of it. I remember the night they finished writing it, all five came pounding on Joni's and my door at like, three in the morning and sang it for us. It was cute to see how excited they were, but at the same time, it was the middle of the night and I kind of wanted to punch all of them in the face.

It is a great song though. I'm looking forward to hearing it again. I'm sure it will be a hit, just like the rest of their singles. Not just because it's a good song, but because they're the ones singing it.

Josh:
Can't forget
The way you looked that night
In a starlight dress
As we walked the velvet air of summertime.

Sam:
Saturn set and Venus danced
Her way across the sky
But I never guessed
That you would feel so right.

All:
You said, "This is a dream,
An enchanting fantasy,
And what is real's
Not what it used to be."
Girl, believe me when I say
Wouldn't have it any other way

Why don't we redefine reality?

This is real to me.
Yeah, this is real to me.

Oliver:
Morning comes
With all the colors of the day
Green and blue
Against the great Apollo's golden ray.

Josh:
But I can't wait to meet again
Beneath the Milky Way
And this time, love,
I hope you're here to stay.

All:
Yeah, this might be a dream,
An eternal reverie,
But sometimes real is
More than what you see.
Girl, what I'm saying now is true
All that's real to me is you
To see you smile is all I'll ever need.

Jesse:
And I believe in everything you are
In a world of constellations, you're my lucky star

All:
If this is a dream,
A beautiful mystery,
Then what is real
Don't matter much to me.

But if it's time for you to go,
I just wanted you to know
You've changed my meaning of reality

Now this is real to me.
Yeah, this is real to me.
You are real to me.

Chapter Two

"So, please, oh, please
Let me take your hand
And tell you that I love you
Can I make you understand?
That in this whole wide world
You compare to none
So I'm begging you, baby,
Please let me be the one."

Song: "Let Me Be the One"
Artist: The Kind of September
From the Album: *The Kind of September*

With the release of the guys' new album just a few weeks away, the entire team has been working pretty much round the clock to promote it. Interviews, online Q&A sessions, the new single, and, of course, new music videos. I love everything about being a member of the guys' team, but I can tell you right now, there is absolutely nothing more fun than shooting a music video with them.

Since Joni and I are technically employees of the band, we've never actually been in one of their videos, but that doesn't make working on them any less of an adventure. Joni is incredibly organized and a real leader, so she's always kind of acted as the band's unofficial manager, even when we were all still in high school. That didn't change after their agent hired a "real" manager. Joni isn't the one who gets them gigs or plans their interviews, but she is the one who helps the guys be where they need to be, when they need to be. She keeps things moving smoothly, which is a flat-out miracle when a group is as busy as and popular as The Kind of September.

I have a much less defined role in the group. When Sam, Cory, and Jesse first decided they wanted to start a band back in high school, I was just kind of along for the ride. I wanted to support them, and, of course, I wanted to be with Sam. I was there when they wrote their first song. It was never recorded, but it does have potential. Unfortunately, the guys all hate it and for the life of me, I can't figure out why. I was there the first time they sang at a school pep rally. I was there when they decided they needed more than just three guys. I even sat in on the auditions they held because they wanted a female's opinion.

Over time, I began taking pictures and playing around with graphic design. Right before our high school graduation, I designed a website for them. Sam watched the entire time, hovering over my shoulder and pointing out what he really liked and what he really didn't like. I usually can't work like that, but he's actually a great person to have around when you have something you need to get done. He was so appreciative that he fetched me drinks and a snack and he even gave me a back massage.

Now they have a whole crew of people to do that kind of stuff for them, but they've kept me on as an artistic and design intern. Even though I'm taking a few college courses online, I've learned more working hands-on with the artists and other team members than I imagine I ever would sitting in a classroom. When I'm not interning or working on schoolwork, I help out with whatever needs to be done. I help set up equipment or run errands or sometimes, as Sam puts it, I act as their source of balance and normalcy.

Long story short, I guess I'm still just kind of along for the ride.

❀♫❀

After a long day of shooting the new music video for *This is Real*, Josh decides that we all need to head back to our hotel, order a pizza, and do nothing else for the rest of the night. I don't think any of us object.

This new music video is going to be amazing, but we're shooting in Southern California, where the climate is uncomfortably warm for mid-November. Temperatures have been hovering around eighty degrees all day. Being part of the crew, Joni and I are able to wear shorts or tank tops or whatever we want, but the guys are totally at the mercy of the costume and makeup department. Unfortunately for them, this video has them all in really nice suits. I was running back and forth in between takes all day, fetching them cold water bottles and those little handheld fans.

But we all agree that in the end, it's all going to be worth it. The director's vision for the video is amazing: lots of colors, stars, lights, and the hottest band on the planet dancing and singing about love and dreams and fantasy. The fans are going to love it.

For now, however, all any of us really want to think about is pizza. Josh is already on his cell phone placing the order as we make the short drive back to the hotel in one of the rented SUVs.

"Yeah, I want four large pizzas, one cheese, one pepperoni, one sausage, and one with the works. Everything you've got. We'd also like... one, two... Jesse's a freak who doesn't like garlic... three orders of garlic bread and do you deliver drinks by the liter? Great. We'll take two Cokes and a Pepsi. You guys want anything else?" he asks us. Joni, Oliver, and Jesse are all in the other vehicle, so it's up to Sam, Cory, and me to make sure all of our dietary bases are covered.

"Do they have dessert?" I ask.

"Do you have dessert?" Josh repeats my question. "They have cinnamon rolls."

"Those," Sam demands, pointing an authoritative finger at Josh's face.

"How about five orders of cinnamon rolls?"

"This is going to be a feast," Sam announces once Josh hangs up with the pizza people.

"Do you think I have time to shower before it gets here? I feel really grimy," I say.

"I'm definitely going to. I'm still picking pieces of whatever that stardust was out of my ears," Josh complains, scratching at his ear like a dog.

"As long as you're not picking it out of your nose," Cory remarks.

"No shower for me. I'm going to skip the soap and make you guys breathe in my stink," Sam teases as he spreads his arms far and wide across the back of our seats. Quite uncharacteristically, I lean out, away from him and his now fully exposed armpits.

"Why are you gross?" I ask him.

"Would you want me any other way?" he asks.

"I'm actually pretty open to the idea."

But of course, that's a lie. I can't imagine him any other way, nor do I want to.

Once we're inside, we all head to our respective rooms for a shower. Joni and I share a room, so I let her go first. She's much faster at bathing than I am. It probably stems from having grown up with a twin brother and being forced to share a bathroom. I have two younger siblings, a brother and a sister, but our schedules were so different that we rarely experienced any bathroom conflicts.

After my shower, I change into my favorite pajamas. Sam actually gave them to me for my twentieth birthday last year. The pants are dark blue and they have little white and yellow daisies on them and they came with a blue tank top.

And no, believe it or not, they actually weren't a random gift. He asked me what I wanted and I really couldn't think of anything, so I just blurted out the first thing to come to mind, which was pajamas. He also threw in a $50 gift card to Target because, come on, who doesn't love Target?

I tie up my long, light brown hair into a ponytail and apply just a tiny touch of mascara even though I know none of the guys care at all what I look like. After two years of working and touring together, we've all seen each other at our worst, and somehow, we all still like each other. It might actually be a miracle.

"Hey, Mel!" Joni pounds on the bathroom door. "Are you done primping yet? Oliver just texted me that the food is here."

"I'm not primping," I insist as I open the door to face her.

I know she doesn't believe me, but she doesn't press the issue. Even though I've never told Joni how I feel about Sam, I'm pretty sure she knows, or at least suspects, that I have feelings for one of the guys. I also know she'd tell me, should I ever decide to act on those feelings, that I was making the worst mistake of my life and that I would be totally and completely miserable. Then she'd say that even if we did end up dating, he'd eventually dump me, and it will make things awkward forever. And then, knowing her, she'd throw in something a little patronizing like, "And I just don't think you could handle that, Mel."

I can understand why. She was really hurt when Jesse broke up with her. He's probably turned her off of dating professional musicians for the rest of her life, which is a little sad, since I'm pretty sure Oliver has a huge crush on her. I actually think they'd make a really cute couple. She's so bossy and outgoing, and he's so sweet and still a little shy despite having achieved worldwide adoration and acclaim. They'd be precious together.

But right now, Joni is too focused on her career (actually, the guys' career) to even think about dating. Unlike me.

"Good. Let's go. I'm starving."

"I am, too."

So we head down the chilly hotel hallway to the room Oliver, Josh, and Jesse are sharing. About halfway there, someone comes running up behind us, places his hands on my shoulders, and jumps. He manages to land on his feet, but he still stumbles a bit and almost face plants right there in the middle of the hall.

"Smooth," Joni laughs.

"Thanks," Sam grins that megawatt grin that will forever make my heart skip a beat. He's wearing his pajamas too: plaid pants and a loose-fitting gray tank top that reveals not only his sexy skinny-guy muscles but also his numerous tattoos. And despite his earlier threats, he's also done us the great favor of showering. His hair is still a little damp and he smells like his classic Old Spice soap.

"I'm glad you changed your mind about making us bask in your natural odor," I tell him.

"I considered it, but then I remembered that male pheromones can sometimes make females go crazy, so I decided to spare you the involuntary primal lust. You're welcome."

"Wow, Sam. Your empathy toward the female plight is overwhelming," Joni remarks.

"As is your humility," I add with a laugh.

"So where's my brother? Or is he already waiting for us?" Joni asks.

Sam and Cory always end up rooming together because Cory is the only one who is willing to put up with Sam's annoying sleeping habits. I swear, the boy talks, he snores, he's a tosser-turner, and when he's really stressed out, he's even been known to sleepwalk.

Once, when we were in junior high, we had this one history project that just about did him in. It was odd, because he was never one to worry about school, but apparently, throughout the course of that project, he woke up in a different room at least four or five times and once even in his backyard. Thankfully, he doesn't get stressed out very often, so he rarely runs off anymore.

Still, that doesn't mean he's a pleasant roommate.

"No, I ditched him after I realized that chatting up his girlfriend has become more of a priority than the basic instincts of our mortal preservation."

Translation: When Sam is hungry, he waits for no one.

"Oh, please don't tell me he's inviting her," Joni groans.

"Probably not. But he might miss out on the pizza if he doesn't get a move on it."

I almost comment that there will be plenty of pizza, but then I remember just how much four hungry twenty-year-old guys can eat. I've seen Sam polish off an entire pizza by himself and still have room for dessert. I don't know where it goes, but he can eat and eat and never gain an ounce. All of them can. It's so annoying. I look at a cookie, I gain five pounds. But not boys.

It's really not fair. They're all already cute and talented. They could at least give the rest of the world the courtesy of having to watch what they eat.

Sure enough, when we arrive, Jesse and Josh are both already on their fourth piece of pizza. Oliver, being quite possibly the politest person I've ever met, has graciously waited for us.

"Hey. Where's the less pretty Foreman twin?" Josh asks through a mouthful of pizza.

"Young Cory has decided to forsake our delightful companionship and fine Italian cuisine for an evening of engaging his new love in electronic conversation," Sam explains.

"You mean he'd rather spend his night talking to a beautiful woman than hanging out with *us*? That bastard!" Jesse pretends to be outraged.

"I never thought I could be so offended," Oliver jokes. "But we should probably still save him a few slices."

"No! It's every man for himself!" Josh proclaims loudly, standing up on his bed. He's in nothing but a pair of boxer shorts and a white undershirt. "Of course, you ladies feel free to help yourselves." He winks at Joni and me.

All the guys are devastatingly charming, but Josh is definitely the biggest flirt. He will put the moves on anyone. He loves to hug, kiss, and cuddle, and he really doesn't care who it is. Joni and I have started keeping tabs on how many sneak-attack kisses we've received from him. I've gotten twelve. Joni's sitting pretty at eighteen. Sam and Jesse are tied at twenty-four, although they're not aware that we've been keeping track.

The fact that Josh has kissed Sam more than I have, I'm not going to lie, is kind of depressing. Of course, Josh's kisses are never on the lips. I'm guessing he reserves that for the girls he actually wants to date. No, the kisses we receive are always on the cheek or on the forehead, or sometimes on the back of the neck.

Cory finally joins us about thirty minutes later. There are a few slices of pizza left, but they're all the small, wimpy pieces that no one wanted. By that point, the rest of us are pretty much stuffed and are all lounging around on pillows while Josh flips through the channels on the television, trying to find something to watch. Sam is lying next to me, and every once in a while, he twirls his fingers through my hair or leans over and pretends he's going to poke me in the ear.

I don't know why, but I don't like people messing with my ears. I never have. If you have a guy friend, never tell him what you don't like, because he will find a way to use it against you. For some reason, they think it's really funny. Or maybe it's their way of getting attention. As for Sam, I think he just gets bored, so to entertain himself, he starts picking on me.

Don't tell him, but I'm secretly okay with it.

"So how is Miss Tara Meeks tonight?" Jesse asks Cory once he's settled in with us.

"She's doing well, thank you," Cory responds cheerfully. "I invited her to come visit the set tomorrow."

"Noooo. Why?" Joni groans.

"Because she's never been on the set of a music video before."

"Neither has the weird smelly guy that sat by me in ninth grade algebra but you don't see me inviting him to visit us on set," Joni counters.

"I want to make a joke about Sam being the weird smelly guy from ninth grade algebra, but I'm too full and tired," I mutter.

"Hey." Sam glares at me. "That's not nice." And to punish me, he sticks his finger in my ear.

Seriously, do any other girls put up with that kind of stuff?

"Cory, do you really think it's very professional to have your girlfriend out here while you guys are on a very strict time schedule?" Joni continues to push the issue.

"Sis, I'm not sure you've noticed, but we're quite possibly the least professional people on the planet."

To be fair, I think that's only partly true. No, they'll never be poster children for modern day professionalism, but as far as musicians go, I think the guys are very professional. They're well-mannered and gracious. They don't stir up drama. They don't get drunk or trash hotel rooms. They're usually pretty punctual. Everywhere we go, everyone always talks about how surprised they are that the guys are so well-behaved.

"My mum thinks we're professional," Oliver comments with a sleepy yawn.

The rest of us snicker, but Joni is still scolding her brother. "You need to tell her that this isn't a date and she's not a part of production in any way. She is strictly a guest and she needs to stay on the sidelines. Do you understand?"

Cory clearly doesn't like being bossed around by his sister, but he also knows better than to try to argue with her.

"Yeah, fine. Whatever you say."

Which is how discussions with Joni usually end.

Chapter Three

"Don't you think
You ought to know by now
How you make me
Crazy, crazy
My heart's racing, racing.
And don't you think
We should be one by now
You know that you're
The only one for me
So baby, don't you think
That maybe we should be
Together now."

Song: "Together Now"
Artist: The Kind of September
From the Album: *The Kind of September*

There's always a bit of a melodrama whenever one of the guys gets a new girlfriend.

First, there's the speculation. He'll be spotted chatting with her backstage, or maybe the paparazzi will catch them leaving a restaurant together. Fans will notice that he's paying her a little extra attention on Twitter or maybe that he posted an extra-friendly picture of them on Instagram.

Then, there's the debate. Are they just good friends? Are they dating casually? Is it all a publicity stunt? Did they have a one-night stand and now she's expecting his child and he's with her only because he has to be? Is it *love*?!

The most controversial part is when the fans split up into teams. They're either very, very super supportive of the couple, in which case they will welcome the new love interest with open arms and post on all their social media sites about how cute they are, or simply, they're not. When that's the case, the girl can, at times, be the target of online attacks, bullying, and gossip.

Then, of course, there are the relationships that the tabloids and the gossip columns make up just because they can. Like a few days ago when rumors were flying around about Sam dating Kelli Barnett, the reality star. It happens to all five of the guys all the time, but for some reason, Sam is their main target. He's actually got something a reputation for being a player, which is ridiculous because he's only had two real girlfriends in his life and neither lasted longer than a few months.

The bottom line is when you date one of the guys, even if you're just reported to be dating one of them, you kind of become famous by default, and not always in a positive way. It shouldn't be that way, but it is.

Josh has always said that he has to like a girl a whole lot to deal with that kind of pressure and publicity. Fortunately for the guys, they're all still very young and most fans understand that yeah, they're going to be dating. They're cute, famous, successful, and could pretty much have any girls in the world. Of course they're going to date.

Unfortunately, not everyone is going to be happy about it. Joni, for example.

Now granted, she's unhappy for completely different reasons, seeing as her brother is the one who invited his girlfriend to set today, but it's still stirring up a bit of drama. When Joni doesn't approve of something, she makes sure that everyone knows it. If you don't agree with her, you're wrong and probably in for at least a few hours of passive aggressive cold-shouldering.

Today, however, there's too much to get done for her to dwell on Cory and Tara for too long.

The guys just got out of makeup and Tim, the director, is going over his vision for the scene they're about to shoot. They're supposed to be following this guy around in a dream-like universe. The guy has fallen in love with this beautiful girl and he's trying to work up the nerve to speak to her. She seems to be aware of his presence, but somehow, she never sees him, leaving the viewers to wonder if one of them might not be real. It's actually a really cool concept.

Right as shooting begins, I notice Tara and another girl walking my way. I'm dressed pretty down but I have my very own name-tag lanyard and walkie-radio, so maybe I look official.

"Hey Joni!" Tara grins.

I turn around, expecting to see Joni standing behind me, but when I don't, I realize Tara is talking to me. It's kind of understandable. The only time she's ever met me, I was with Joni, and we do sort of look alike. Well, not really. But we both have brown hair.

"Oh, um. Hi. I'm not Joni," I tell her. It's a little unnerving to talk to her. She's 5'11, five inches taller than me, and so beautiful it's kind of like looking into the sun.

"Oh, I'm sorry. Who are you again?"

"It's okay. We've only met once. I'm Melissa Parker."

"Huh. I don't recognize your name," Tara's friend comments.

"Oh, I work behind the scenes. I'm not famous or anything." It's weird, but I almost feel like admitting that to these girls is like admitting that I don't wash my hands after I go to the bathroom.

For the record, I always wash my hands. But I stand by my point.

Sure enough, Tara's friend replies, "Aw, that's cute."

Okay.

"So, Meredith, do you know when Cory will have a break?" Tara asks. I'm guessing she's talking to me since, you know, we're the only ones standing there.

But *Meredith*? Really?

"Um, no, I don't. They just started. But I can show you around and introduce you to the team if you'd like."

"Oh no, that's fine. We're just here to see Cory. Oh, and Sam," Tara exchanges a playful smirk with her friend.

You know that feeling when your blood runs cold and your heart speeds up and you get that weird tingling pain in your face? It's that feeling when you know that something you really don't want to happen is about to happen.

Yeah, that's what I'm feeling.

"You know Sam?" I ask, hoping they can't hear how out of breath I suddenly sound.

"No, but I promised I'd hook her up," Tara says with a devious wink. "Oh, I guess I forgot to introduce you."

"Gee, thanks. Some friend you are," the girl teases.

"Meredith, this is my good friend, Courtney Vickers. She and I are represented by the same agency, but she's also considering a career in music, which is *part* of the reason I brought her today."

"Yeah, the other part is because my bestie Tara told me that she could get me an all-access pass to Sam Morneau," Courtney nudges Tara's shoulder and giggles. It's only then that I become aware of just how gorgeous *she* is. She's not as tall as Tara, but she's still taller than I am. Her hair is a rich and luscious auburn and her perfectly mascaraed eyelashes are what I think people refer to as starburst blue. Three different shades of blue, but amber around the pupil. I've always envied eyes like that.

Part of me isn't worried that Sam will go for her. He can usually see right through girls who are actively trying to get famous. But another part of me realizes that Sam is only human, a male human at that, and male humans are often

26

seduced by female humans, especially the ones who look like Courtney Vickers.

❀♫❀

After two hours of shooting, Tim finally tells the guys to take a lunch break. Cory heads right over to Tara and Courtney. Much to my dismay, so does Sam. I'm hoping he's just going over to say hello. Sam is, by far, the friendliest person I've ever met. Of course he's going to go say hello to his friend's girlfriend.

"So, who's the new girl?" Oliver asks, taking a seat next to me at one of the lunch tables.

"Courtney. Tara's friend. Hoping to hook up with Sam." I try to act like I don't care. Which I don't. Not really. You know, in an alternate universe.

"Ah." Apparently, he's not surprised.

"Oh my God, I'm starving," Josh says loudly, as he and Jesses sit themselves and their sandwiches down across the table from us.

"Hey, who's that girl with Tara? She's hot." Jesse comments.

I'm going to get tired of this question.

Thankfully, I see Sam bid Tara and Courtney a cheery goodbye as he makes his way over to the makeshift sandwich buffet. By the time he finally joins us, he's already eaten half the food on his plate.

"Does anyone have any napkins? I've got cheese powder under my fingernails," he announces, his mouth full of Doritos. Courtney should see him like this, in his natural state.

"Why don't you just wipe it on your pants like you always do?" I ask.

"Because Tiffany said if I ruin one more of her outfits, she's going to kill me," Sam says. Tiffany is their stylist and is always getting after him for being messy. Well, all the guys are messy, but for some reason, Sam is the only one who ever gets in trouble for it.

"Here." Oliver passes a few napkins over to Sam.

"Oliver, you're a lifesaver."

"Or at least a pants-saver." Jesse laughs.

"Almost just as important," I comment.

"So, Sam. You want to tell us about Tara's friend? Courtney?" Josh asks, waggling his eyebrows suggestively.

"What about her?" Sam asks with a laugh that might mean he's either amused, embarrassed, or potentially smitten. I'm hoping it's one of the first two. Disgusted would be even better, but he rarely gets disgusted by anything. Except sponges.

"Did you get her phone number? Her address? Are you going to teach her what it means to really be a woman?"

"Josh, ew." I glare at him.

"She just gave me her number," Sam tells us. By now, I'm pretty sure he's embarrassed. Despite his well-established reputation as a ladykiller, Sam still gets so bashful about the idea of girls liking him or wanting to date him. It's funny, because he's so wild and crazy and he definitely puts on a good show of making people think he's sexy. But the second someone actually tells him that, he's like a shy little turtle.

"Are you going to call her?" Oliver asks.

"And if not, do you mind if I call her?" Jesse asks.

"You know what, this sandwich is just amazing. It's like the best sandwich I've ever had in my life," Sam remarks, stuffing his face with food once again.

"So, the video looks like it's going to be good," I offer.

"It is. I think I'm going to tweet about it," Jesse says, whipping out his new smart phone. "Oh hey, looks like Tara's already telling the world that Sam has a new girlfriend."

"What?" Sam and I exclaim at the same time.

"On set of new #TKOS music video with the BF #CoryForeman and BFF #CourtneyVickers hitting it off with #SamMorneau. Winky face."

"Oh, this will be fun," Sam mutters.

"That's just ridiculous. She just met you! You didn't even talk for that long! You're not her property!" I hiss.

"Wow. You know Sam, if you're unhappy about it, you should sic Melissa on her. I think she's about ready to tear her head off," Jesse smirks.

I can feel the blush creeping up my cheeks, but I try my best to act casual.

"I just think it's wrong for her to run around spreading gossip about you that isn't even true," I tell them.

"Most gossip isn't," Josh reminds me.

Before I can think of a witty comeback that would portray me as a protective friend and not a jealous girl with a really pathetic crush, Cory, Tara, and Courtney are standing over us.

"Well, I think we're off. We had so much fun on set today. Thank you so much for having us," Tara says.

"Oh, it was our pleasure," Oliver replies.

"Oliver, you're too sweet," Tara grins. "And Sam, I told Cory that the four of us need to double sometime, and he totally agrees."

"Definitely," Cory says. "I think it'd be fun."

"Oh. Okay yeah, sure." Sam blushes. My heart sinks a little, but I'm fairly certain he's just being polite. "It was nice to meet you, Courtney."

"Likewise," she smiles and pauses to lay a seductive hand on his shoulder. "Call me any time. I'd love to sing for you sometime. You might even be able to talk me into a private performance."

Josh can't help it. He bursts out laughing and has to bury his face in his arms. I would be laughing with him if the whole situation wasn't so awkward.

At this point, I don't think Sam's face could possibly get any redder. I think the only time I've ever seen him blush harder was the time the button on his jeans popped when we were in high school. See, this button didn't just fall off. It flew off. Like, his pants were so tight that the button literally could not hold on for a second longer so it launched into the air like a rocket. And maybe, if that was all that happened, it wouldn't have been so embarrassing for him. But the button, in its flight to freedom, accidentally hit a girl that he had a crush on in the eye. It hit her so hard that it left a welt. Poor Sam was mortified, but the rest of us all thought it was hilarious.

Let me tell you, I have never felt worse for laughing until I cried.

"Sounds fun," Sam finally replies. "I'll see you around."

"I'm going to hold you to that," Courtney points at him before Cory escorts them off set.

"Oh, that poor girl," Jesse smirks.

"What?" Sam asks.

"You're not going to call her. You're not even going to follow her on Twitter. I can see the headlines now. *Yet Another Heart Broken by Notorious Ladies Man, Sam Morneau.*"

"Didn't you just break up with Whitney Preston a few weeks ago?" Oliver asks.

Whitney Preston is an actress who most recently appeared in the big screen adaptation of a popular young adult book about time travelers and dinosaurs. Sam has never even met her.

"What can I say? It wasn't me, it was her," Sam jokes lightly. Despite his good-natured approach to the rumors that follow him everywhere he goes, I know his media-inflicted reputation bothers him. He's a good guy with a huge heart and yeah, he's kind of weird and gross and there's his bizarre thing with sponges, but he'd never intentionally hurt a woman or lead her on. None of the guys would.

30

"Guys," Joni appears out of nowhere.

"Hey, where have you been?" Oliver asks.

"Yeah. You missed your best friend forever, Tara," Jesse remarks.

"Yes, that was the whole idea," Joni says. "You have five minutes to finish eating and get yourselves together for the next scene. Mel, if you're done, I want you to go grab one of the handheld cameras and start shooting some stuff for the behind-the-scenes video."

"Right." I love filming. It's one of my favorite on-set jobs. It's especially fun because it gives the guys a chance to just be themselves in front of the camera. In the music videos, you'll see them singing and dancing and being all charming, but behind the scenes, they get to laugh and joke and just be guys.

As soon as I have a camera, I make my way around set, filming the crew, the props, the set itself, and of course, the guys. At one point, Josh runs straight at the camera, takes it in his hands, and kisses the lens.

"That one's for you," he grins, winking at the camera.

"You just left a lip smudge on the lens," I laugh.

"Oops. Here you go." He raises his elbow as if to polish the lens with his sleeve, but I take a step back, just in case he's actually planning to do it.

"I'll clean it," I assure him.

Next, I find Jesse in front of a mirror, running his hands through his hair and making sexy, come-hither faces at his reflection. Fans will love that.

"You look beautiful, I promise," I tell him.

"Hey. Go away. This is private," he teases, cozying up to the mirror.

"Not for long it isn't."

"Don't judge me, Melissa. I've seen you. I've seen you and your little hairbrush and your Maybelline eyeliner and your Revlon lipstick. Speaking of, why do you use two different brands?"

"I think the real question is why do *you* know which brands I use? I don't even think I knew that."

"Because infidelity is *wrong*, Melissa. It's just plain *wrong*." Of all the guys, Jesse is the only one who calls me Melissa. I don't know why. Maybe that's how I introduced myself to him. Everyone else just calls me Mel.

"Glad to hear you say that, Jesse. Do you have anything else you'd like to share with the fans?"

He stares straight into the camera. "I love you. Desperately. Passionately."

"Almost as much as he loves himself," I quip.

"That's it. You're gone. Out," he orders.

I wander a bit further. Oliver and Cory are both back in makeup, so I film them for just a moment before taking off in search of my favorite member of the group.

I find him off to the side, lurking behind one of the green screen panels that have been set up for dream sequences.

"What are you doing?" I ask.

"I have a Dorito stain on my shirt and I'm hiding. Shh!" he holds his finger up to his lips and looks frantically at the camera. I have to laugh.

"What happens when you have to go film?"

"I haven't thought that far ahead yet!" Now he's laughing too.

"You're going to get in so much trouble..."

"I know. Tiffany's going to ground me or something."

"Can she do that?"

"Probably!" he cries, his big blue eyes bugging out.

"Maybe you should bring like, an adult bib or something for these days you have to eat in costume."

"Or I could just take off my shirt," he grins seductively at the camera. Then he begins to do a strip-tease.

See, this is what's strange about him. When no one is actively hitting on him, he's one of the flirtiest guys you'll ever

32

meet. Actually try to flirt back, however, and he transforms into a shrinking violet. It just doesn't make sense.

"I'm not sure the Internet is ready for this," I tell him. Of course, I'm actually very much enjoying it, especially once the shirt fully comes off and he starts swinging it around and shimmying up to the camera.

And naturally, it's right at that moment that Joni comes rounding the corner, wondering what the hell we're doing.

"Nothing, nothing," Sam throws his shirt back on and begins to button it. He'll never admit it to her, but Joni scares him almost as much as Tiffany. Before he follows her back to the group, he leans into the camera and mutters, "You can slip the money into my G-string later."

Yep. That's the Sam I know and love.

Chapter Four

"And I said, baby
I want to make you love me
Want to let you hold me
Want you to stay with me,
And baby,
You know I'd leave you never
I want you for forever
So please, baby, let's not fight
Everything will be alright
You're the one I need tonight
Please, baby stay with me tonight."

Song: "Stay With Me"
Artist: The Kind of September
From the Album: *17 Times Over*

One week.

We have one blissful week off before the release of *Meet Me on the Midway*. The guys are taking that time to spend with their friends and family that they don't get to see while they're out on tour. I'm taking the time to catch up on my Marketing 2301 homework.

When I first broke the news to my parents two years ago that I was forgoing the traditional college route in order to run around with a group of guys who like to sing and perform and, let's face it, wear pants about two sizes too tight, they weren't overly enthusiastic. Granted, I was eighteen and I didn't need their permission, but as their daughter, I still wanted their approval.

They knew what a great opportunity working with the guys would be for me. After all, how many people can say that they're in the inner circle of a famous band? It's given me the chance to travel the world, meet people, learn new skills, and earn a living doing what I love with the people I love. I'm extremely thankful for that, and so are my parents.

However, they still lamented the fact that I wouldn't have a "normal" college experience. I could understand that. They met in college. They've both often said that college was the best time in their lives (apart from welcoming their wonderful, gorgeous, brilliant children into the world, of course). They don't want me to miss out on anything. That's where our compromise comes in. I agreed to take online courses. I don't take as many as I would as a full-time student, but I've gotten at least a few English and history credits out of the way. I'm dreading math, but hey, Sam is actually really good at it. Maybe he can help me out.

I actually haven't seen the guys or Joni very much at all this week. We've texted, but for the most part, everyone's kind of doing their own thing. Josh and Jesse have been hanging out with friends from high school. Oliver has been spending a lot of time at home with his family and his dog. Cory, apparently, has been Skyping non-stop with Tara, who thankfully stayed in LA while the rest of us flew back home to the Bay Area. And Sam, as far as I know, hasn't left his house and has been binge-watching Netflix, eating home-cooked meals, and sleeping.

Of course, the tabloids are telling a different story.

Sam Morneau - WASTED!

Mega-heartthrob and member of the popular boy band, The Kind of September, Sam Morneau was spotted early Friday morning, leaving a club in Downtown San Francisco with friends. The young singer, who is under the age of 21, appeared drunk and disheveled as he tripped and stumbled his way out into the streets and into a waiting car...

"This is so stupid," I mutter as my mom sits down next to me on the couch.

"What?"

"Nothing. Just dumb rumors."

"Is it about Sam?" Mom asks. I look at her. I'm shocked to see that she looks concerned, almost nervous.

"Mom, you don't actually believe that he would do this, do you?"

"No, Sweetie, of course not. I know Sam. He's been a good friend to you for a very long time. It's just... well..."

"What?" I demand.

"This isn't the first article to be written like this. And they seem to be appearing more and more - "

"Mom, they're lies!" I can't believe she's saying this to me. She knows Sam! She's known him since we were little kids. How could she even suspect that any of these awful reports are real? "I promise you, none of this is true. These are just stupid gossip columnists and phony reporters trying to make a buck. Sam is still the same guy, I promise you."

"I know, Melissa, and I believe you," she says, scooting closer to me. "I'm just a little worried about what you're being exposed to."

"What do you mean?"

"I mean... You've been out there for two years now. I know you can take care of yourself. You're smart and you've experienced so much more than I had at twenty. You've done more than I have even now. I just want to make sure that it's an appropriate atmosphere for you. You're still so young. If you're being exposed to anything indecent or - "

"Mom!" I leap to my feet. This is ridiculous. "I know you're trying to protect me, but please, hear me out. The guys are not what the media makes them out to be. I don't know why these people think it's okay to make up stuff like this, but they do. It's nothing new. It's been happening to singers and actors and other famous people for years, and it's going to keep happening. But you can't believe everything you read."

"I know that. But I'm your mother. I worry. Can you really blame me?"

"No," I sigh and sit back down.

"The truth is, honey, I know how you feel about Sam. I know he's your friend, but I also know he's more to you than that. And I just... the last thing I want is to see you get hurt." Her voice and her eyes, the same shape and color as mine, are completely sincere.

As much as she loves Sam, I know there's also part of her that resents him for not liking me back. She's felt that way ever since he and the guys decided to skip our Senior Prom to go perform a last-minute show after we'd all agreed to go as a group. Joni and I decided to ditch Prom as well to accompany them on their gig. It actually turned out to be a pretty fantastic night anyway, but I'll admit, I still would have liked to have had one dance with him.

"Mom, he's not going to hurt me. I promise."

"I hope so, sweetheart. Because you deserve the world."

"I love you," I say and wrap my arms around her shoulders, breathing in her warm, familiar perfume. It smells like my childhood, and like home.

"I love you, too."

Every time we come home, Sam's mom, Laurel, invites everyone over to celebrate and to just enjoy some down time together. Laurel has always loved hosting parties, even before Sam bought her her dream house in Marin County. Now, she loves hosting them even more, but with Sam on the road so often, she claims she never has much of a reason to throw one.

For the party, I prepare my famous peanut butter chip brownies. They're Sam's favorite. I'm not much use in the kitchen most of the time, but I have to admit, I make some damn good brownies.

By the time we arrive, the Foremans and the Berkleys are already there. I'm not sure Jesse's family will make it. They live up near Napa. But I'm sure Josh and his parents will show up.

Sam is waiting to greet us even before we make it to the door. Somehow, he looks extra handsome whenever he's home. He's wearing dark skinny jeans and a loose, white button-down shirt. His hair is messy as ever and his broad smile is absolutely contagious.

"Welcome!" he exclaims, throwing his arms out.

I go in to hug him, but Mom gets there, first. I guess she's gotten over whatever reservations she'd had about me being around him earlier.

"Sam, it's so good to see you!" she tells him.

"You too, Mrs. Parker." Even though Sam's mom insists that we call her Laurel, Sam has never felt comfortable addressing anyone else's parents that way.

My brother and sister are next. To my little brother Aidan, Sam is the older brother he wishes he had. He's seven, and in his eyes, Sam is a regular superhero. My little sister, Brooklyn, however, is just about as taken with Sam as I am. She smiles shyly up at him and giggles when he asks her how she's doing. At thirteen, all of her friends listen to The Kind of September, but she is incredibly modest about having grown up with several of its members.

After them, my dad claps a hand on Sam's shoulder and says, "Looking good, son."

"Thank you, Sir." Sam is always so polite to my family.

Finally, it's my turn to greet him. Even though we've texted, I haven't actually gotten to see him in almost a week. That's not okay.

Instead of a smile or a hug, however, he just stares down at the platter in my hand.

"Is that what I think it is?" he asks.

"Maybe," I tease.

"You are my favorite person on this planet," he says and finally pulls me into his arms.

There, in his warm and sturdy embrace, I can't help thinking, *Likewise*.

After he lets me go, he takes the brownies from me ("I don't trust you with them," he jokes) and leads me inside, where everyone is hugging and greeting one another. Joni is by my side in an instant.

"Thank God you're here," she remarks.

"What's going on?"

"I'm just tired of listening to my brother run his mouth about Tara and how he wants to bring her home for Christmas and how Sam really needs to consider going out with that Courtney girl because she really, really, really liked him. Of course she liked him. He's Sam Morneau. Everyone likes him!"

"Do you think he'll really bring her home for Christmas? That's kind of a big step and they really haven't been dating that long."

"Right?!" Joni agrees. "I don't know. I just thought of all the guys, Jesse would be the one to pull some stupid stunt with a model. Or Josh. Or even Sam. I'd have expected any one of them before my brother."

"I think Sam's smarter than that," I say.

"Oh come on, Mel. I know you two have like, a thing or whatever, but he's a guy. And guys are stupid."

I want to ask her what she meant by *a thing*, but Oliver approaches us before I get the chance.

"Hey, stranger," he greets me with a one-armed hug.

"Oliver, you should be honored," I tell him.

"Oh? Why's that?"

"According to Joni, you are the only decent member of the entire band. Come to think of it, you might be the only decent member of your entire species. And by species, I mean men."

And just like that, Oliver blushes like crazy. It's so adorable. I wonder how Joni would react if she knew how he felt about her. Even though she's basically sworn off singers, performers, and celebrities in general, I'm secretly hoping she'd make an exception for Oliver.

"I didn't say the others aren't decent. But I do think you're the only one smart enough to know better than to date a stupid, shallow clout-chaser."

"Hey!" Sam appears, looking thoroughly offended, even with a mouthful of brownie. "I'll have you know that the last girl I dated was very smart."

"That's because you were in Kindergarten and she got a gold star for drawing a pony," Joni remarks.

"She set the bar pretty high," Sam jokes.

Sam actually has dated since Kindergarten. In fact, he's had two fairly serious girlfriends. The first was a girl we went to high school with named Cameron Griffith. She was really smart and, if I hadn't been so jealous, I'd almost go so far as to say they were kind of cute together. But she was a real perfectionist and over-achiever and she didn't like the idea of dating a guy who wanted to be a musician. The second was a girl he met after the band released their first album, an aspiring singer named Joyce Berlin. She was actually pretty talented and I think has gone on to record her first EP. Anyway, she was his first and only real high-profile relationship, regardless of what the tabloids would have readers believe.

After Josh and his family arrive, Laurel escorts all of us outside to her beloved backyard. It's her absolute favorite part of her new home. She has an amazing garden of rosebushes with buds of every color. She's also decorated the bushes and fence with white twinkle lights. I've always thought that her backyard, with its bright colors, sweet smell of flowers, and overall sense of serenity, was like a little piece of Heaven on Earth.

We eat in groups at the white steel tea tables she has set up. For what will be our last night with our families together until Christmastime, Laurel has prepared rotisserie chicken, rosemary potatoes, green beans, and an amazing assortment of breads and rolls. It's a bittersweet event to be sure, but the food is *incredible*.

In the middle of dinner, Josh's dad stands up, holding his wine glass in the air.

"I'd like to propose a toast," he says with a goofy grin that is practically identical to Josh's. You can totally tell that they're father and son. Everyone stops talking and turns to look at him. "First of all, to all of us here tonight. Our wonderful friends. I can't tell you how honored I am to be a part of this extended family."

The group responds with, "Hear, hear!"

"Next, to our talented sons - and daughters - and all the hard work they put in to making their dreams come true."

"Cheers!"

"I'll drink to that!"

"And finally, to the new album! You all are stars. And we couldn't be more proud of you."

It's only then that everyone begins to applaud.

"Wait, wait!" Sam rises, holding up his glass of water. "I'd like to add thanks to all of you, our parents, our families, for supporting us."

"Hear, hear!" all of the kids cheer.

"And most importantly, to the fans. I don't know if they'll ever know how much they mean to us, but without them, we wouldn't be here. So, here's to them."

"To the fans!" Josh yells.

"Cheers!"

Sometimes it is easy to forget, living in such a tight-knit bubble, that there are other people in the world. Maybe because, working in the background, we really don't see too much of them. But to the guys, the fans are absolutely everything. I'd even go so far as to say they care about the fans more than their own well-being. I think that's one of the reasons why people love them so much. They're themselves, they're appreciative, and they absolutely adore and cherish their fans.

Once we've all finished eating, we disperse again into small groups. Josh is off sharing crazy stories and stupid jokes with the parents while Sam and I are back with Oliver, Cory, and Joni who, like before, is dominating the conversation by griping about Tara, tabloids, and other distractions.

I have to admit, I've been tuned out for a while when I feel someone lean into me.

"Want to go for a walk?" Sam mutters in my ear, his breath hot on my skin. His very proximity makes me feel like I've just been struck by ten-thousand volts of electricity.

I glance up at him, his handsome features soft and subtle in the violet glow of early nightfall, and I find I can only nod.

Without telling anyone where we're going, we slip out the side gate to the alley and around to the sidewalk. We used to walk together to the playground together all the time when we were younger. On occasion, we'd race (he'd always win) or exchange tidbits of useless information that we'd, for some reason, bothered to learn over the years.

Most of the time, however, we'd just talk, which is why I end up asking, "Are you okay? Do you have something on your mind?"

"Nah. I just wanted to get away from the drama," he nudges me playfully. He knows I know exactly what he's talking about. "And it's such a nice evening. I just kind of wanted to enjoy it. One last night before the chaos starts up again."

"I know what you mean," I say. "Well, sort of."

"No, you definitely do. You work just as much as we do, and you take classes on top of it. Speaking of, did you finish your assignments?"

"I did. Now I just have the final exams, which I don't think should be too hard. They're scheduled for the week the album is released, though, so it'll be a bit hectic. But it'll be fine. It always is."

"You're so smart. It'll be a breeze for you," Sam grins at me.

"Eh, we'll see," I smile, wondering if he'll ever know how his compliments affect me. "What about you? Are you ready for it all?"

"Oh yeah. It's what I love. I am going to miss this, though. This time away from the cameras and the craziness. It's nice to just be here at home," he says, glancing around at the trees, the houses, the California sky over the distant hills. "Then again, I can't wait to get back on the road, spending nights in hotels and on the tour bus, being on stage... Those are the moments I live for, you know?"

"Yeah, I do. I just wish the media would give you a break."

He shrugs. "It's just a thing. I can deal with it."

I know he can. Sam is strong, much stronger than I am. I hate the lies and gossip that are spread about him. If any such thing had been written about me, I'd go crazy. Sam is actually a really good influence on me in that respect. Every time I think to get angry or upset, he manages to calm me down and put things in perspective. I've never met someone with such a positive outlook on... everything.

Near the end of our walk, a couple of young girls who can't be any older than six or seven approach Sam with their mom. He smiles and greets them like just seeing them has made his entire night. They both give him huge hugs and he graciously poses with them for a picture that their mother snaps on her smartphone. Then, he signs autographs for each of them before wishing them a goodnight and sweet dreams.

And he's supposed to be the wild-partying ladies' man.

Chapter Five

"Spinning, spinning round
Until the world begins to fade
And I don't think I'll live to run
Or see another day
Her love, it leaves me on the ground
While she falls away
17, 17, 17 Times
17 Times Over..."

Song: "17 Times Over"
Artist: The Kind of September
From the Album: *17 Times Over*

This morning, we're all awake bright and early to catch a flight to New York, where the guys will spend most of their time being interviewed by talk shows, news outlets, and just about every person with a microphone.

After emotional goodbyes and promises to call our families as often as we can, the entire group, bandmates, musicians, security, managers, all of us are escorted to a private waiting area where we all spread out immediately to wait for our flight.

Something that the guys have always strived to emulate is individuality. When Josh and Oliver first joined, they expressed concern than as a part of a boy band, they might be viewed as "clones," and although they wanted to present themselves as one team, one band, they also want to be known as themselves. They don't dress alike. They put their own spin on their choreographed routines. They're five guys in one outstanding group, and none of them ever have a problem being who they are.

For example, all five have drastically different relationships with early mornings.

Jesse is the one who has to be physically dragged out of bed, and once he actually is up, he has to have some sort of coffee or energy drink before he can force himself to talk or have any kind of human interaction. Honestly, though, it's kind of his fault. He and Josh are total night owls and they're the ones we always have to shush whenever we all sleep in the same room or on one of the tour buses. But at least Josh is pleasant in the mornings. That boy falls asleep with a smile every night and he wakes up with one every morning. He's just a great person to be around all the time.

Except when it's 2:00 AM and you're trying to sleep after a twelve-hour work day and he won't stop laughing or making weird noises.

Then there's Cory, who is more of a morning person than anyone else I've ever met, except perhaps his sister. They're both highly ambitious and motivated people, but they seem even more so when they first wake up. That's probably why Cory gets so many things tossed at him at times like these. While the rest of the guys are relaxing, trying to steal a few extra winks, Cory likes to discuss their plans for the day. This morning, however, he seems too preoccupied with his phone to care about what the others are doing.

Oliver, surprisingly, is probably the worst of the bunch. He's sweet and adorable most of the time, but he can actually get a little snappy when he's tired. I told you that Josh and Jesse will be the ones being shushed late at night? Well, Oliver is always the first to do the shushing. It's more of an issue at night than in the morning, but if he hasn't gotten a proper night's rest, he can be just as crabby in the AM.

We'd never admit it to him, but both Joni and I agree that cranky Oliver is actually really precious.

Finally, there's Sam. Sam in the morning has always reminded me of a sad, sleepy puppy. His eyes get droopy, his hair is always a disaster, and he usually wears something like sweatpants and a hoodie. He barely talks, and when he does, his voice is hoarse and much lower than it normally is. He's never in a bad mood, but I don't think he fully wakes up until at least an hour later.

As for me, I'm not a morning person, but I can usually wake myself up and get myself together fairly quickly. Unlike Sam, Jesse, and Josh, who are already camped out and dozing, I'm hanging with the awake crowd consisting of Oliver, Cory, and Joni.

"One day, I'm going to go buy a giant teddy bear and plant it on Jesse, I think," Oliver remarks.

"That would be so funny," I say. It would be, too.

"Yeah. Then I'm going to post it on Twitter, Instagram, and Facebook. In fact, we might just make it the new album cover."

"I'd buy it," I tell him.

"Yeah?"

"Definitely."

"I'd buy the teddy bear," Joni remarks.

I realize I should probably be taking this rare and limited down time to study for my upcoming final exam, but I feel like I spent the majority of my week off doing school work. Now, I just want to spend time with my friends and prepare for our next adventure.

By the time we board, Josh, Jesse, and Sam are finally awake enough to at least act like functioning members of the human race, if not society. I happily take an aisle seat next to Sam and Jesse. The whole group knows that I'm something of a nervous flyer. That's why I usually prefer life on the tour bus to hopping around on airplanes. That bus might be cramped and crowded and more often than not, it smells like a strange mix of cologne, stale popcorn, and a mountain of men's dirty socks, but at least it stays on the ground.

Then again, sharing that one itty-bitty, teeny-tiny bathroom with all of them might just make it a toss-up.

Life on the road with the hottest band on the planet? Not glamorous. But you know, at least they're entertaining.

"Say cheese!" Sam announces and holds his smart phone up to take a selfie of Jesse, him, and me.

"Are you tweeting that?" Jesse asks.

"Nope. This one's just for me." Sam takes a lot of pictures. He has this fancy camera that he's absolutely in love with, and he takes it everywhere he goes. Right now, however, it's packed up and stowed away with the rest of our luggage, so he has to resort to snapping pictures on his phone.

"Good. I look horrible," Jesse murmurs and runs a hand through his messy, auburn locks. Somehow, even though he in no way intended for it to be so, he makes it look like a seductive gesture. That's probably why, next to Sam, he gets the most attention from girls.

When the plane finally starts to move, the flight attendants step out to begin going over safety procedures. I've heard the drill so many times that I could probably recite it from memory. Besides, with the plane preparing for takeoff, I'm trying my best to stay calm and not let my flight jitters get the best of me.

Sam knows that I'm nervous. Every flight that he sits next to me, he offers his hand during takeoff. I always take it. Today is no exception. As the plane turns onto the runway, he lays his hand down on the armrest between us, palm up and fingers slightly spaced apart. I take it, and immediately, flying doesn't seem that scary at all.

Okay, I'll admit that there is a small part of me that always tries to get a seat next to Sam just so I can hold his hand like this. Holding hands with him is one of my favorite things in the world. But the fear of flying is still there and is, in fact, a real nuisance when I'm not sitting next to him.

"You okay?" he asks me.

"Yep. Great," I reply, sounding breathless. Thankfully, as far as he knows, that's because I'm stricken with terror and not because his fingers are currently laced through mine.

"Melissa, I can't believe you made it through that flight to Australia last year," Jesse remarks.

"Easy. I took a Dramamine."

"There you have it. She was unconscious," Sam laughs.

The rest of the flight is relatively uneventful. Jesse dozes off again, his head resting against the closed window, Sam listens to music on his phone, and I bury my nose in the newest Meg Cabot book. The others like to make fun of my young adult literature addiction, but hey, at least I read. I bet you anything that right now, Josh is playing a video game, Oliver is watching Netflix on his iPad, Cory is messaging Tara, and Joni is griping about it.

I ask you, who is the cultured one in this group?

❀♫♩❀

Once we land in New York, we're given twenty minutes for lunch before the guys are whisked away to the dressing rooms for a day of interviews with a host of reporters from a variety of news outlets. They're the kind, you know, where the interviewers sit down one at a time with the guys in a dark room with an enormous picture of the new album cover in the background. Most of the time, they ask questions about the album, sometimes touring, and sometimes it gets personal, even downright silly.

For example, "Who's the biggest prankster of the group? Who is most likely to kiss and tell? Whose feet smell the worst?"

The answers to those questions, by the way, are Josh, Jesse, and Josh again. Sam's feet are a close second, though.

Today, however, I'm guessing most of the questions will be about the new album and the upcoming tour. Fans, of course, are ecstatic, as are the guys. They're always excited to talk about their new music.

Joni and I only see them for a brief moment before they meet with the first reporter, but they all look great. By now, they've each established their own individual look. Jesse is the sexy rock star. Oliver is cute and stylishly nerdy. Cory is a throwback to the late 90s. Josh is dreamy in an All-American kind of way. And Sam is trendy and a little rebellious.

The interview, as expected, starts with questions about the new album. What are their favorite songs? How long did it take to write? Is this their best album yet?

Then come the personal questions, or as this reporter puts it, "the questions that millions of girls around the world want to know the answers to."

For instance, "What do you look for in a girlfriend?"

Josh wants a girl who likes to laugh and is into sports. Oliver likes girls who are smart. Jesse isn't sure, but he wants to be able to talk with her about anything. Sam's answer is my favorite. He says, "I want her to be my best friend. I want to know she loves me for me."

I hope for a fleeting moment that maybe, just maybe, he's talking about me. But I know, deep down, that if he did have feelings for me, he would have said something by now. Sam's not a shy guy. He's also not very subtle. He's so very caring and he always wears his heart on his sleeve. If he has feelings for someone, he's going to let her know.

Finally, it's Cory's turn to talk about his ideal girlfriend. Of course, he responds with, "Well, I'm kind of dating mine right now."

"Oh, please," Joni scoffs.

"What?" I ask.

"Tara Meeks is not his ideal girlfriend. She isn't anyone's ideal girlfriend."

"Joni, why do you hate her so much?" I ask. I mean, yeah, she is kind of stuck-up and a little rude, but to be honest, I'm sure other male celebrities have dated a lot worse.

"I've told you. She can't get famous on her own so she's using my brother - no, she's using all of them - to make a name for herself. She doesn't care about him. And he just doesn't see it. He doesn't know what this is doing to the entire band."

"The guys seem okay with it. I mean, I don't think they're big fans or anything, but they seem to at least be happy for him."

"I'm not talking about how they feel about it. I'm talking about the fans. The media."

"What do you mean?" I ask.

"I've been talking to Stan and a few of the other crew members. They think that with the album release and the tour coming up, it's better for the band's image and their relationship with fans if the guys at least appear to be single," Joni explains. Stan, for the record, is the band's manager. He's the one who, basically, runs all of our lives.

"Wait, what?" This is the first I've heard of that, and I've got to be honest, it doesn't make much sense to me.

"Why are the guys so popular, Mel?"

"Because people like their music."

"Of course there's that, but think about it. Most of the fans are girls. Young and single girls. And Stan thinks that those fans would be more loyal to a group of guys who are, for all intents and purposes, unattached. Personally, I don't think that's giving the fans enough credit, but at the same time, with all the tabloids trying to stir up drama, I can't help but think he might have a point. Reports of bad behavior and rude girlfriends are huge turnoffs for some fans. And they should be!"

"So, Stan doesn't think the guys should be dating at all?" That's news to me also.

"I guess if they dated someone halfway decent, it would probably be okay. But if they do, I think he would definitely prefer that they keep it on the down low. And if I'm right about Tara, which I'm pretty sure I am, she wants to make it known as far and wide as humanly possible that she is dating Cory Foreman. It's sickening."

"So, is that why you don't want to date any of the guys?" I ask, thinking of Oliver.

"No, it's because I'm not into workplace relationships or guys who are constantly in the spotlight. We watch from the sidelines, but just imagine what it must be like to actually date that. No privacy. Constant gossip and speculation. It'd be horrible."

"But if you really cared about him, don't you think it'd be worth it?"

She looks me in the eye. "Exactly who are we talking about here, Mel?"

"No one," I try to shrug it off. "I'm just being hypothetical."

I've said before that I'm pretty sure Joni knows I'm harboring a secret crush on one of the guys. In fact, she probably knows it's Sam. She grew up with us, too. I'm sure she's seen the way I act around him. Maybe she's pretended not to notice in order to spare my feelings. But that would go against her God-given instincts to tell me what to do, which would probably be to forget Sam Morneau altogether. That, or maybe I'm just a better actress than I've been giving myself credit for all these years.

The guys end their long day of interviews with an acoustic performance of *Highway*, their second single off the new album. Although they usually have a band backing them up, I think they sound just as good, if not better, when it's just them singing along while Jesse plays guitar. It reminds me of the days when they were first starting out.

Those were some of the best days of my life.

Sam:
Lost in time
Tell me what's real
This place, it never changes

Oliver:
Time to get lost
I'll take the highway
Don't want to know where I'm going
But I'll tell you when I get there

All:
Gonna take my time
Roads keep stretching on
And I've got everything to find
I'm leaving tonight
Please don't miss me when I'm gone
Everything will be alright

Jesse:
Under the sky
I see myself
This face, it's seen the ages

Cory:
Can't stay below
I'll take the highway
I'm not going to turn around
But I'll think of you when starlight fills my eyes

All:
Gonna take my time
Roads keep stretching on
And I've got everything to find
I'm leaving tonight
Please don't miss me when I'm gone
Everything will be alright

Josh:
And I can't promise you
That I'll come back to stay
But I will remember
Oh I will remember
Promise you'll remember

All:
Gonna take my time
Roads keep stretching on
And I've got everything to find
I'm leaving tonight
Please don't miss me when I'm gone
Everything will be alright.

Chapter Six

"I wanna wake up to your smiling face
Wake up to your arms around me
Why does this night have to end?
Tell me, why has morning found me?
If I have to wake up, wake up
Please let me wake up, wake up
With you."

Song: "Wake Up"
Artist: The Kind of September
From the Album: *Meet Me on the Midway*

To get the fans excited for the new album and the world tour, the guys have written a short book. It's called *The Tour Bus Diaries* and it's filled with all of their stories and personal experiences from the road. Some of the entries are kind of short. Some are longer. Some are insightful reflections. Some are rants. Most of them are pretty hilarious. All in all, it's the guys' way of sharing a little bit of themselves with the fans. It's their way of thanking them for always being there.

The book also includes a lot of pictures from behind the scenes that fans have never seen before. I actually took a few of them on my phone. All in all, it's a fun book and I really think that fans will enjoy it.

To celebrate the release of *The Tour Bus Diaries*, the guys are participating in a big meet-and-greet book signing at one of the New York convention centers. The event sold out within minutes.

We arrived at the convention center early this morning, long before any of the fans or media representatives showed up. Well, there were a few of the more passionate fans staked out near the back entrance where the guys were escorted in. Despite Stan and security trying to hurry them along, the guys lingered back, took pictures, and signed a few early autographs.

Now the guys are getting ready to head out to the signing table. Joni will be standing out with them to monitor the crowd and to keep everything moving efficiently. We only have three hours and we, especially the guys, want to make sure that every fan gets a chance to interact with them. As for me, I'm once again on camera duty. Just photography for today, though. No video. And that's okay.

It's always interesting to see fans reactions to actually meeting the guys. Some of them scream. Some of them break down and cry. Some can't stop talking. Having known them as long as I have, I've never been starstruck by any of them (well, except for Sam... and that was even before he was famous). However, I know for a fact I'm not immune to the fangirl phenomenon.

Case in point: last year at this big international music awards thing, I ran into this really hot Irish singer-songwriter and I kid you not, I could not remember how to breathe. His eyes were just so blue and his accent was so dreamy... I think I rambled on about how beautiful he was and how much I loved his music for a good five minutes before he finally determined I was psycho and walked away. Oliver told me that he felt the same way when he was introduced to Emma Watson. It happens. Of course, when it happens to Oliver, he still comes off as adorable. With me, it's just creepy.

Plus now I know that if things don't work out with Sam, I definitely don't have a shot with the hot Irish guy.

As the next group is escorted in, I can't help but overhear a conversation a few older girls are having.

"He's so sexy. I just hope that those rumors about that one girl aren't true," the first one says. She's tall and wearing turquoise skinny jeans which are actually really cute with her black and white top. I don't know who she's talking about, but if it involves rumors, I can only imagine it's Sam.

"They probably are. I mean, it was pretty much confirmed by Cory's girlfriend," says the second one, a blonde with black glasses and a purple scarf.

"God, I can't stand her. Have you seen the way she talks to fans on Twitter?" their third friend asks. She's wearing a pink dress and gray boots. Why do all these girls dress cuter than I do?

"No. I un-followed her and Cory after she said that designers shouldn't cater to anyone bigger than a size four," the first one mutters.

"What a bitch. I can't believe Cory would go for someone like her! He's just so sweet. I mean, I never had a crush on him, I'm totally an Oliver girl, but I always thought Cory was really smart and sensitive. Why would he put up with someone like that?" the second girl demands.

"Because she's gorgeous and looks matter," the third one grumbles.

"Oh well. At least we still have Sam," the first girl sighs.

"Maybe," the second girl reminds her.

"No, I know Sam. He's better than that. He'd never do that to his fans because he loves us too much," the first girl replies.

"You know one of these days, he will get a girlfriend," the third one says.

"Of course he is. It's going to be me," the first girl says with a laugh.

"Oh, whatever." The second girl rolls her eyes as they're called forward to meet the guys.

Whatever hard feelings they had completely melt away as the guys smile and ask them how they're doing. All three of them are squealing, and the third one is even jumping up and down. The first one ends up getting a big hug from Sam, which shouldn't make me jealous, but come on, who wants to see the guy they like hugging another girl? Especially one who has just pretty much professed her undying love for him?

I tell you, sometimes I think life would be so much easier if I'd just fallen in love with an accountant.

Compared to most days being a working member of The Kind of September's inner circle, today was kind of easy. For the guys, the book signing was actually pretty low-energy, which is a rare occurrence for them. It's true, they had about a thousand different conversations with a thousand different fans (maybe not that many... I don't think we had that many books), but at least they got to stay seated most of the time. Of course, Josh is moaning about his wrist hurting from signing so many autographs, and Sam keeps saying they're all going to end up with carpal tunnel by the time they're twenty-two, but I think they all had a lot of fun.

Now, Sam, Oliver, and I are sitting out on the balcony watching the sun set over the New York skyline while the others are inside watching movies.

"I can't believe the others are missing this," Sam remarks, shooting a photo with his camera. The sun has just disappeared beneath the horizon and the city lights are growing brighter and brighter against the hazy orange and maroon backdrop of the darkening sky. I've watched the sun set from countless balconies all over the world, and yet somehow, it always feels like the first time.

"I know," Oliver says. "Growing up back home in London, I always dreamed of visiting New York City. It was my one goal in life. Make it to New York. Now, I've made it dozens of times and I'm still dreaming of it. I actually have been thinking of buying a home for meself here."

"You should. Then we'd all have a place to stay," I grin.

"Hey, we should all just move in with Oliver!" Sam announces.

"Yeah! We could be like the Brady Bunch!" I laugh.

"Except minus the weird sibling relationships and retro seventies hairstyles," Sam adds.

"I don't know. I think I could sport a bowl cut," Oliver says.

"Yes, you'd look absolutely smashing, Love," I grin, mimicking his accent. Sometimes, Oliver's British roots come out more than usual, and more often than not, we like to tease him about it.

"Besides, no one should ever sport a bowl cut unless they're named John, Paul, George, or Ringo," Sam says.

"Ringo is my favorite," I say as a bit of an afterthought.

"But George is your favorite musically," Sam adds on. Oh, he knows me. I mean, that's the number one quality you look for in a guy, right? Being able to correctly identify your favorite Beatles?

"I thought girls liked Paul," Oliver mutters.

"But Ringo has the best personality," I insist.

"How do you know? You never met him."

"She has a thing for drummers," Sam smirks.

"Shut up, I do not." This is one of our *things*, but it's one that, honestly, I could live without. Long story short, when I was a junior in high school, I went to a music banquet with one of the drummers from marching band. He wasn't exactly the best date ever. He talked a lot, but he didn't seem to care about anything I had to say. He also had really bad acne and got a little handsy as the night progressed. He claimed it was because I was "taller" than him, but that's no excuse. Needless to say, I don't look back on that night with very much nostalgia. Just a bit of contempt. And nausea.

58

"Really? Do you have a thing for Chris?" Oliver asks. Chris Ortega is the band's drummer. He's a great guy, but for one thing, he has a girlfriend. For another, he watches really weird cartoons and they kind of freak me out. And finally, I have a thing for someone else. Coincidentally, the one teasing me about my thing for drummers.

"No, I do not have a thing for Chris. I don't have a thing for drummers!"

"That's good. Because, I think Angela might be able to beat you up," Oliver tells me. Angela is Chris' girlfriend, and she's really tall and used to wrestle recreationally in college. She could totally beat me up. Thankfully, she's also really sweet and she and I get along pretty well.

"Then I guess it's a good thing I don't have a thing for drummers."

"Methinks the lady doth protest too much," Sam remarks in a sing song voice that is nowhere near as sexy as his regular singing voice.

"Methinks you're about to get punched in the face," I counter.

"You wouldn't hit me. I'm too pretty."

"Wanna bet?"

And so I do hit him. Not hard, and definitely not in the face. But I punch him playfully on the arm. He, in turn, goes to grab my ear but I slap his wrist away. For some reason, this makes him laugh and he reaches over his chair to try to tickle my ribs, resulting in me almost tipping over in my lounge chair and spilling my glass of water all over myself.

"Oh! Oh my God, that's cold!" I shriek. It's also November in New York, which makes it even colder.

"Mel, I'm so sorry." I don't know if he's actually sorry or not. He's laughing too much to tell.

"Let me get you a towel," Oliver stands up and rushes inside. Technically, Sam should be the one rushing to get me a towel since, let's be honest, this is all his fault. But I can't say I mind being left alone on the balcony with him, overlooking the magnificent glow of the lights of New York City.

Even if my pants are cold and soaking wet.

"I really am sorry, Mel," Sam apologizes again. This time he really does sound sincere. Though he is still kind of giggling. "Are you okay?"

"I'm fine," I say. To be totally honest, I'm still laughing too. And shivering slightly. He notices.

"Here," he says, slipping his jacket off and tossing it over me. It's warm and leather and it smells like him. I love it.

I also love just being out here with him, almost to the point where I'm wishing Oliver wasn't coming back. Part of it was because I love being alone with Sam no matter what, but I especially love being alone with him here, in this city. There's something about New York. I can't explain it. It's less of a place and more of an experience. To see it and to hear it is all to feel it. It's the feeling of adventure and being away from home and being totally free. The city lives and breathes and thrives and its energy stays with you long after you leave it.

It's a place to lose yourself and, I realize looking into Sam's smiling face, it's a place to dream.

Chapter Seven

"Baby, I just wanna dance with you
Take you in my arms and make you mine
You know I've never seen your eyes so blue
And I never knew that this could feel so right
You tell me that the world is calling you
Well, baby it can wait while
I just wanna dance with you."

Song: "Dance With You"
Artist: The Kind of September
From the Album: *The Kind of September*

From the very beginning, the guys have wanted their fans to know that they come first. One of the ways they ensure that is by staying as connected to them as possible. During their very first tour, they started doing these monthly question and answer sessions on YouTube. As their career advanced and their lives got more and more hectic, however, they were only able to get the videos out a few times a year.

Today, they've got a little extra down time so they decided to film a new video from our hotel. One of the things I admire most about the guys is that even when they have free time, they're using it to work, write music, or connect with their fans.

They're arranged around a couch with a fantastic view of New York City behind them and they've all got huge grins on their faces. This is the kind of thing that they really love, partly because it reminds them of when they were first starting out. They still love everything about what they do, but the crazy schedules and constantly being in the public eye does take a toll. They're also a lot more relaxed and free to be themselves in this setting than they usually are in interviews.

"Alright, let's get this show on the road!" Sam exclaims, clapping his hands together. "Mel, are we recording?"

Oh yeah, they've asked me to film.

"Almost. Is everyone ready?" I ask them. I get five variations of yes and two thumbs up. "Then we are rolling in three, two, one..." I give them a nod as I press record.

"Hello, Internet!" Sam greets their future viewers with a cheerful wave.

"Greetings, earthlings," Jesse says in a weird nasal voice which I guess is meant to sound like an alien. Every once in a while, he decides he wants to try to be funny. Between you and me, he's better as the sexy bad boy.

"What's up, what's up, everyone?" Josh grins. "We are here in New York City, as you can see behind us." All five guys turn around to look at the city. "And we wanted to bring back something that we haven't done in far too long."

"Questions and answers!" All five shout out together.

"As you all hopefully know, we have a new album coming out soon," Cory says.

"But not soon enough!" Josh cuts in.

"And that's why we're here today," Oliver concludes. "Why don't we get started?"

"Alright, our first question is from Rochelle in Phoenix, Arizona," Sam reads from the laptop that they're sharing. "Her question is, 'If you could star in any television show or movie, what would it be and why?'"

"*Star Wars*," Josh answers immediately.

"Why would you pick *Star Wars*?" Sam asks him.

"The real question is why *wouldn't* I pick *Star Wars*?" Josh rebuts.

"Okay then. Oliver?" Sam asks.

"I want to be the next Sherlock Holmes."

"Because you're British?" Jesse asks.

"Yes. That is the only reason," Oliver deadpans.

"I'd like to play someone smart, like a doctor or a professor. I can't think of a name though," Cory says.

"That sounds so boring. It's so you," Josh remarks.

"I'd be in a horror flick, like *The Shining*," Jesse answers, looking cool and confident.

"But you hate scary movies," Sam reminds him. *That* is the understatement of the century. Jesse might like to pretend he's a badass or whatever, but the truth is he is a huge wimp. Last Halloween, we decided to have a classic horror movie night on the tour bus and Jesse flat-out refused to watch *The Exorcist*. According to him, he "accidentally" saw it as a child and it scarred him for life. Now, I have no idea how you "accidentally" see a movie, but clearly, it was a traumatic experience.

"I know, but if I was in one, then maybe it wouldn't be as scary," Jesse explains.

Okay, so he's not very good at being a bad boy either.

"I'd be in zombie show, like *The Walking Dead*," Sam finally answers. "And I say that because zombies are cool. Also, I really like the idea of being a survivalist."

"Says the guy who just bought a new pair of seven-*hundred*-dollar shoes," Cory comments.

"Um, excuse me, my *mom* bought them for me and they're for the tour," Sam says. By this point, I have to bite my tongue to keep from laughing.

"Fair enough."

"Alright, what's the next question?" Oliver asks.

"Oh, this is a good one," Jesse says. "How did you guys come up with the name The Kind of September? That's from Lora in Edinburgh, Scotland."

"That is a good question," Cory agrees. "We actually got it from a musical that Sam and a few of our friends saw back in high school, *The Fantasticks*. One of the songs in it is called

Try to Remember and it's actually a quote from that song. We all just really liked it."

"Both the name and the song," Sam adds. "It's actually a great musical too."

"Would you go so far to say that it's *fantastic*?" Josh asks, nudging Sam's arm with his elbow. "Huh?" He follows up with a huge wink and a cheesy grin.

Oh, Josh. Aren't you just so funny?

"Okay, our next question comes from Meagan in Hot Springs, Arkansas. I love that place," Oliver grins. "The question is if you could switch places with any of your bandmates, who would it be?"

"You," Sam answers.

"Me?" Oliver sounds surprised to hear him say that. "Why me?"

"Because all the girls just totally love your accent."

"It's true," Jesse says.

"In that case, I want to be Oliver too," Josh says.

"Same here," Cory agrees.

"Okay, so we'd all be Oliver. Oliver, who would you be?" Jesse asks.

"Josh," Oliver replies.

"Really?" Josh looks like that one response just made his entire life.

"Yeah. You're just so happy all the time. And I wish I could make people laugh like you."

"Oh, Ollie... I don't know what to say." Josh pretends to cry and waves his hand in front of his face.

"Okay, our last question comes from Savannah in Pensacola, Florida," Cory says. "She asks, 'Is it hard being away from your friends and family for such extended periods of time?'"

"Oh wow, that's a heavy one," Jesse says.

"The short answer to that is yes, it's very hard," Oliver says. "But I think it's also worth mentioning that we have some of our very best friends here on this journey with us, and I don't know what they think, but I feel like we've become a family."

"Definitely, I've always felt that way," Josh says.

"Same here," Sam chimes in.

And even though I'm not a part of this video chat, I have to agree with them. There are a lot of hard things about being on the road and away from home, the first of which being you don't really feel like you have a home anymore. Of course you have a *home*, as in the place you grew up, but you don't really live anywhere. You also have to be really okay with just going with the flow and eating whatever you have in the hotel or the tour bus instead of sitting down for a nice home-cooked meal of your choice. Everyone is busy and stressed and together twenty-four hours a day, so if you have even the slightest argument or problem, you'd better get over it quickly because you are going to be seeing that person all the time.

But when it all comes down to it, families are kind of the same way. In fact, sometimes, I think that's what makes a family. It's so easy to be around people when everything is... well... easy. But the people who've been with you through thick and thin, who've seen you at your absolute worst, and who still want to hang out with you at the end of the day?

If that isn't family, I don't know what is.

It's snowing.

It's only November and it's already snowing. A lot.

Okay, it's November in New York. I'm guessing this isn't as much of an unheard-of phenomenon as it would be in say, San Francisco, but for a group of twenty-somethings who are from San Francisco (well, and one from London), it's a weird experience.

Maybe not so much for the Londoner, but for the Californians, it's weird. That's probably why we're all making such a big deal out of it.

The second the snow started falling, Sam scrambled for his camera and ran out onto the balcony to take pictures. About five minutes later, however, he remembered how much he hates the cold and ran back inside. He's been repeating the same pattern for about three hours now.

Josh, on the other hand, announced that we all needed fleece blankets, hot chocolate, and a fire. Apparently, experiencing a real New York winter is a lifelong dream of his and he wants to do it right. Unfortunately, Josh, Jesse, and Oliver don't have a real fireplace in their hotel room, so we had to improvise. As it turns out, there's a cable station that, around this time of year, is a non-stop video of a fireplace burning and Christmas music playing in the background.

True, it meant we couldn't watch a movie, but since the seven of us (actually eight... Cory has invited Tara to join us later) can rarely agree on what we should watch, it's not a tremendous loss. Especially since, after making us all hot chocolate, Jesse broke out his acoustic guitar.

So this is what we're doing on a snowy, northern night. We're all in our warmest pajamas and covered in fleecy blankets. We're drinking hot chocolate by a pixelated fireplace. And we're singing acoustic radio hits from the 1990s and early 2000s. It might be one of my most favorite moments of all time.

Especially when Sam scoots up beside me and pulls me into his fleecy, blanketed arms.

"I'm cold. Hold me," he mumbles in a silly voice that is somehow still insanely cute. So I happily oblige, linking my arms through his and snuggling up against his side. "You know what this makes me think of?"

"What?" I ask.

"When we were kids and we built that enormous blanket fort in your living room."

"That was up for like a year."

"I know. It was kind of our secret clubhouse."

"That wasn't a secret at all."

"That's true," he acknowledges as Jesse begins to strum another familiar tune. "Breakfast at Tiffany's" by Deep Blue Something. Classic.

Unfortunately, just as we're about to sing the chorus, Cory's cell phone rings, interrupting what may have actually been the best performance of the evening.

"Oh! Take five, crew. That's Tara! I'm going to run downstairs to meet her." And with that, Cory bolts out the door.

"He's going to be running awhile. We're on the fifteenth floor," Josh remarks.

"Can I ask you all something?" Joni asks hesitantly. "What do you guys think of her? Honestly."

"She's a little abrasive, but I don't a problem with her," Oliver says. Of course he doesn't have a problem with her. Oliver is the nicest guy alive. He doesn't have problems with anyone. Except for when it's too loud for him to sleep. Then he has problems.

"I'm not her biggest fan, but she seems to make Cory happy," Sam answers.

"Does she still think you're dating her friend?" Jesse asks Sam.

"I don't know," Sam sighs.

"She won't be thinking that long when she sees you cuddling the camera girl," Josh smirks. Of all of the guys, he's always been the one to call us out for our strange relationship. Granted, it wouldn't be so strange if we were actually dating.

"It's okay. She has no idea who I am," I assure them.

"What?" Sam asks.

"It's true. She thought I was Joni."

"Huh. That's rude," Sam remarks. Then he notices the death glare that Joni throws him. "No. Being mistaken for you personally isn't rude. It just seems rude that she doesn't know who everyone is by now."

"I think she has her mind on other things," Jesse smirks.

"Yeah. Like using my brother to get famous," Joni scowls.

"Come on, Jo, you really think that's the only reason she's with him?" Jesse asks.

"You don't?"

"No. I think she's with him because he's a nice guy. He's talented. He's not as handsome as me, but let's be honest, who is?" At this, several eyes roll. "All I'm saying is you need to give Cory a little credit."

"You know, Jesse, I'm sure you mean well, but I really don't need *you* lecturing me on - "

But before she's able to complete that sentence, the door opens and Cory appears with Tara in tow.

"Hi, everyone!" She gives an excited wave.

Everyone replies at once.

"Hello, Tara."

"Hi."

"What's up?"

"Oh my God, my life is just so crazy right now. Like, you have no idea," Tara says taking a seat in between Cory and Josh.

"Oh, we might," Josh laughs.

Tara ignores him and keeps talking. "First, I'm doing this huge shoot for this national campaign for a makeup line whose products are designed to enhance a woman's natural beauty. So it's like, you're wearing makeup, but it doesn't look like you're wearing makeup."

"So what's the point?" Sam laughs.

It's only then that Tara glances up at him and notices him and me sharing our large plaid fleecy blanket. And she definitely doesn't approve.

"The point is to make women proud of their natural beauty." She looks at me. "Who are you?"

"Um, I'm Melissa. We met at the video shoot a few weeks ago..."

"Oh, right." I'm not sure if she actually remembers or if she's just throwing me a bone. "Well you know, Sam, Courtney is still eager to get to know you a little better. I know she'd be happy to go out with you if you'd give her a call." Now she sounds like a football player on the offense. Not that any of us (except maybe Josh, who was super into sports in high school) actually know what an offensive football player sounds like.

"You know, Tara, that's awesome, but I just... I don't think I have the time to date right now," Sam says. Good. Good excuse. I mean, it's actually kind of true. But that's beside the point.

I hope I don't look as smug as I feel.

But Tara is just not letting it go.

"Oh, she doesn't mind. She doesn't have a lot of free time either, what with her modeling and trying to launch a singing career. I know she'd love to just get together with you, maybe pick your brain on music. So do you want me to let her know that you'll call her once you're back in Cali?"

Sam sighs. He hates it when people put him on the spot.

"Honestly Tara, I'd really rather you didn't," Sam tells her.

"What? But she really, *really* liked you."

"And I liked her. She seems like a great person. It's just that - "

"What? Is she not good enough for you?" Tara suddenly rounds on him.

"No! It's not that - "

"Then what? Not pretty enough? Or are you just not interested in a woman who knows her own value?"

"What?

"I've read all those articles about you. How you prefer your women loose and vapid - "

The next thing I know, Sam and I are both on our feet. Sam, looking irritated and yet still somewhat apologetic, seems lost, like he doesn't know where to go or what to do. I, on the other hand, am shaking with all sorts of disgust and anger. Even though I never, ever resort to violence, my hand is balled into a fist, ready to fly right into those perfect pearly whites and cosmetically altered nose.

Thankfully, Sam's bandmates are still calm enough to remember to use words.

"Hey!" Jesse snaps. "Come on, now. No, Sam isn't perfect, but none of us are. You can't believe that crap that goes around on the Internet."

"Yeah, come on, Babe. You know Sam isn't like that," Cory tells her, sounding like he's trying to talk sense into a toddler throwing a tantrum.

"Well, from what I've seen, I wouldn't be surprised," she sneers.

That does it for Sam.

"You know, I think I've had about all the fun I can handle for one night. I'm going to bed. Goodnight," he bids us, making his way toward the door.

"What? But we haven't made s'mores yet," Josh reminds him, holding up the bag of marshmallows.

Sam doesn't respond. Instead, he walks right out the door, closing it quietly behind him.

"I think I'm going to call it a night too. See you all in the morning," I say, following Sam into the chilly hotel hallway. I know exactly how Tara will interpret that, but I really don't care what she thinks. Especially after what just happened.

Sam is already halfway down the hall, so I have to sprint to catch up with him. He turns when he hears my footsteps approaching him.

"Hey," he says. "You didn't have to leave."

"You think I *wanted* to stay with that?" I ask.

He manages a grin. "I guess not." His blue eyes are still as bright and beautiful and cheerful as ever, but I can tell that he's bothered by everything Tara said.

"So, are you okay?"

"Oh yeah, I'm fine. I just didn't want such a good day to end like that, you know?"

"Definitely. Still, you didn't deserve that."

He shrugs. "Comes with the job, unfortunately."

"But that shouldn't be an excuse. No one should have to put up with that, especially someone who hasn't done anything wrong." I'm talking really fast now. It's not a first. I always ramble when I'm upset.

Sam grins and rests his arms on my shoulders like we're at a middle school dance. "I love that you're so protective of me."

I blush. "I'm protective of all of you. I hate it when people try to tear you down."

"You know that's never going to happen, right?" he assures me.

"It better not."

His smile broadens across his face. "So, are you going to bed now or...?" he trails off.

"I don't think I'll actually sleep for a while. I'm kind of jittery. I'll probably just go and read or maybe sketch a little."

"Want to go back to my room and watch a movie instead?"

I love watching movies with Sam, partly because he's so entertaining while he's watching movies and partly because there's a very good chance I'll end up leaning against him again.

And here I thought this night was going to end badly.

Chapter Eight

"She sings to me that melody
Of diamonds on piano keys
The tune of painted harpsichords
And gold viola strings.
And she sings to me the song of night
Of planets, stars, and velvet skies
The word around us fades away
And she has roses on her mind..."

Song: "Roses"
Artist: The Kind of September
From the Album: *Meet Me on the Midway*

As usual, Sam and Cory's room is a horrific wreck. Well, Cory's side of the room isn't too bad, but Sam's side looks like a tornado tore through the room and scattered all of his dirty laundry, snack wrappers, and empty water bottles everywhere. I truly pity the housekeeping staff.

"Sorry it's kind of a mess," Sam apologizes. I have no idea why. It's not like I haven't lived on the same tour bus as him and four other dirty, smelly guys.

"Sam, how long have I known you?" I tease. "It actually doesn't look too bad, you know, considering it's *you*."

"At least I picked up my dirty underwear," he grins.

"Yeah, and I'm only detecting a hint of old sweat socks." I'm only somewhat joking. I'm telling you, twenty-year-old guys are not charming. Like, at all. Not even the super dreamy celebrity guys. They stink just as much as any other twenty-year-old guys. Heck, they probably stink worse because they think they can get away with it.

But hey, at least he changes his underwear.

"That's man smell, baby. Take a good whiff." Sam laughs, acting a lot more like himself now that he's away from Tara and her trash talk.

"But why do men have to smell like wet bath towels?"

"Why do women have to smell like flowers?"

"Because everyone likes flowers."

"What if someone's allergic?"

"Then I'd think they'd like the flower perfume more since they can't stop to enjoy the smell of the actual flower without sniffling or sneezing."

"What if someone's allergic to the perfume? What if they're allergic to everything?"

"Then they should probably see a doctor and get some steroids or something."

"Oh. I was going to suggest they outlaw perfume," Sam remarks, flopping down onto his bed.

"I thought guys liked the smell of perfume," I say, taking a seat next to his head.

"Guys like the smell of new cars and bacon."

"So, you'd rather a girl smell like machinery and breakfast food than flowers or coconuts?"

Sam shrugs. "I don't really care what she smells like. As long as she's a decent, down-to-earth person and I don't have to hold my nose when I'm around her, I think we'll get along pretty alright," Sam says, smiling up at me from his back.

"Are you going to return the favor and bathe every now and then?" I ask.

"Only when my pits start to mildew." His grin is cheeky and mischievous.

"Ew! Okay. We're done here." I hold my hands up in surrender.

"We're done when I say we're done," he announces in some weird monster voice and grabs my foot.

"No!" I shriek and pull both my feet away from him. I'm so, so, so ticklish, especially on my feet. And he knows it, so he shows no mercy.

"What about you?" he asks, probably realizing that I could very well kick him in the face if he tried to tickle me. "What do you look for in a guy? I mean, aside from him being a drummer?"

"For the last time, I do not have a thing for drummers!"

"Okay, okay," he grins. "Seriously, though. I don't know if you've ever told me what you really think about dating."

Uh, yeah. That's because if I were to talk about it, he'd realize that I was describing *him*. Honestly, though, I don't know how I've gotten away with it for so long. Maybe it's because I'm so open with my celebrity crushes (like the hot Irish guy). Or maybe it's because Sam has been operating under the assumption that I'm asexual. Whatever the reason, I've always been pretty good at dodging the What-Do-You-Look-For-In-A-Guy question.

Until now, that is.

"Well, I definitely like a guy with good hygiene." And do you know what Sam does? He laughs. He actually *laughs*. Granted, I meant it to be a bit of a joke, but seriously? The boy is rolling around and holding his sides because he is laughing so hard. This is not funny. "*What?*" I demand.

"Of all the qualities that matter to you in a significant other and you go for *hygiene*?"

"Yes! I know you like to joke about it, but honestly, can you imagine dating someone who didn't wash their hair? Or brush their teeth?" I shudder at the very thought.

"Okay, fine. I guess hygiene isn't the *worst* quality you could have come up with," he acknowledges. "What else?" Why? Why couldn't he have just been satisfied with *hygiene*?

"Well..." Okay. This could get tricky. Just stay calm. Keep it together. Most importantly, remain totally neutral. "He's got to be able to make me laugh. I couldn't be with a guy who wasn't funny."

"See, that's better. Hygiene. Pfft. Hygiene is for the weak."

"No, hygiene is for the man of my dreams." Of course, he doesn't know it, but he *is* the man of my dreams, and apparently, he scoffs at hygiene.

"So, I guess that means that we're all out of the running," Sam remarks lightly.

That one little comment just about gives me a heart attack. What exactly is he asking me? Is this his way of wondering if I'd ever consider dating one of them? Or more specifically, him? No, he's probably just joking, or teasing me for having such ridiculously high standards. Wanting a man who showers regularly and doesn't smell like a gym bag. Imagine that.

Still, the longer I sit here in silence, the sooner he's going to realize that I am, in fact, hiding something and that the truth is that I would date him in a heartbeat if he asked.

But what does he *want* me to say? *Oh, buck up, Pal.* *You've still got a chance. More than a chance if you catch my drift.*

Yeah, like that's gonna happen.

"Don't sell yourselves short," I finally say. "Your hygiene isn't *horrible*."

"I feel like you're only saying that out of politeness," Sam laughs.

"Hey, when you shower, you smell amazing."

"Well thank you, Miss Parker. That means a lot, especially coming from you." Okay, now I know he's teasing me. "But seriously, how would you feel if one of us wanted to date you?"

Why is he pushing this? Is it because of what just happened with Tara? Or is he fishing around for one of his bandmates? Oh, God! Please don't let that be the case. I

75

don't think it is. Cory sees me as a sister. Oliver likes Joni. I'm not nearly hot enough for Jesse. Josh is a huge flirt, but he flirts with everyone! Besides, the girls he usually goes for are the spunky, sporty type, which I am definitely not. I'm more into scarves and coffee shops and cool photographs.

That just leaves Sam. I guess it could be possible that he thinks of me as more than a friend. I mean, we are totally alone in his hotel room. But he's my best friend. It's not like this is a first or anything.

So why am I having such a hard time being honest with him? I want to tell him. I should tell him. Maybe if I told him and he felt the same way...

But what if he doesn't? That would be so embarrassing. Worse, he might begin to feel awkward and uncomfortable around me, and that's the last thing that I want. The entire world is expecting something from him. He is in the public eye no matter what he does. There are very few people he acts like himself around, and I'm honored to be one of those people. I don't want to lose that because I misunderstood his intentions in asking me how I would feel about dating one of them.

Being a girl is so confusing.

"I don't know," I tell him. I wonder if he can hear my voice shaking. I definitely can. "It - It'd be a little weird, don't you think?"

To be totally honest, I have no idea why I just said that. It's like while my brain was debating what it wanted to say, my mouth decided to just spit out whatever the heck it felt like. And for the record, whenever my mouth decides to act on its own, it usually ends up getting me in trouble. Or at least into a situation that I will more than likely end up regretting later.

For instance, by insisting that dating one of the guys would be, and I quote, "a little weird," I may have inadvertently sabotaged any minuscule chance I had of becoming Sam's girlfriend. Yay me.

"Yeah, probably," he agrees. But is he agreeing because he thinks that's what I want to hear, or because he agrees that it would be weird if I dated one of them?

Unfortunately for me, it's probably the first one. I've been told on more than one occasion that guys don't think like we do. Where we will over-analyze and examine every word, breath, movement, and detail, guys tend to think more along the line. For example, they wouldn't give a second thought about the same two-worded text message that would send a girl into a massive spiral of panic and excruciating self-doubt.

Of course, Sam is the one whose best friend is totally lying to his face about being in love with him even though he's told her on multiple occasions that she's one of the few people that he trusts to always be honest with him.

On the other hand, guys just might have it harder. They have to put up with us.

I guess that awkward answer has effectively ended our conversation about dating since Sam props himself up on his elbows and reaches for the remote control.

"So, what do you want to watch?"

Note to self. Late night talks about relationships combined with two hours of zombie flicks make for a terrible, and I do mean *terrible*, night's sleep.

For one thing, it took me forever to get to sleep because I was obsessing over what I'd said to Sam about how it would be weird to date any of them and how he probably interpreted that (re: I think it would be weird to date *him*). For another thing, once I finally did manage to fall asleep, I had zombie and dating nightmares all night.

In the first dream, Sam had asked me out on a date and of course, I'd said yes, but he'd turned into a zombie right as we were about to kiss, so that sucked. Then during the second dream, all of us - the guys, Joni, even Tara - were barricaded inside this small run-down shack in the middle of nowhere.

We knew that zombies could be out there anywhere and it wasn't any sort of the fun that Sam thinks it would be. It was all terrifying. That dream ended with Josh actually turning into a zombie and me having to be the one to kill him. Of course, I didn't have a gun so I actually had to find a long metal rod to impale his brain with. Let me tell you, it was really awkward seeing him at breakfast this morning.

Tonight, the guys are performing at a music charity gala to benefit arts and music education across America. It's something they're wildly passionate about, even Oliver, who only spent a few years of his education in the American public school system. They all insist that those classes really sparked their interest and inspired them to do well in school. It's an issue that I'm afraid tends to get overlooked in the grand scheme of things. After all, there are arguably far more important problems to address.

But when you think about it, a nation's students are its future. The kids of today are tomorrow's leaders and visionaries. They need a well-rounded education, not a system where making the grade is all that matters. Who cares what they memorize if they're not actually learning? That's something that worries me about the decline of the arts in education. Students are treated more like numbers and data instead of young human beings with working, independent minds. That's why music and art and literature are so important. They remind us of what we can accomplish with a little passion and dedication.

The event tonight is a fancy black-tie affair. All the guys are wearing designer outfits that all probably cost more than my childhood home. Okay, maybe I exaggerate, but even after two years, I still can't get used to the lifestyle that comes from associating with the rich and famous. That being said, the guys do look pretty amazing. Sam especially. He's in black skinny slacks, a loose white button-down shirt, and a charcoal gray vest. The rest of the guys are dressed somewhat similarly. They have a little say in what they wear to these kinds of things, but a lot of their wardrobe comes directly from their stylists.

Joni and I, on the other hand, have a little more freedom. She's chosen a traditional little black dress and strappy stilettos that could probably put someone's eye out if she's not careful. Joni is actually quite coordinated. I'm the one who has to watch wear she steps. I wouldn't go all the way to say I'm a klutz, but I have yet to figure out how to walk in heels without looking like a drunk toddler. For that reason, I am in white flats tonight. They go well with the white flowing dress I'm wearing. My hair is tied up in a loose, elegant bun with gold and white headbands. Joni told me that the outfit makes me look like a Greek goddess, which is a pretty awesome compliment.

If I'd had any doubts about Oliver's crush on Joni, they all melted away after I saw the way his jaw dropped when we met the guys down in the lobby of our hotel. The way he looked at her was adorable, and she's so completely oblivious. Now that we're actually here at the benefit, he keeps stealing glances at her. I might have to talk with him about this.

The gala is incredible. There are at least a couple hundred people, all dining on filet mignon, or grilled salmon and scalloped potatoes around candlelit tables. I chose the filet mignon and it might be the best dinner I've ever had in my life.

"By the way," Sam says to me out of nowhere, "you look really beautiful tonight."

It's funny how five simple words like that can totally and completely make a person's day. I hope I don't look as giddy as I feel. I can definitely feel my cheeks flushing.

"Thank you," I reply. "You look quite dapper."

Really, brain? Dapper? Here's the guy I've been in love with for forever sincerely telling me that I look beautiful and I go with *dapper*? Maybe I really would be better off in the event of a zombie apocalypse. Then I could show my appreciation and affection by stabbing his infected bandmates in the head instead of blurting out the first stupid phrase to come to mind.

Fortunately, Sam grins and adjusts his vest. "Dapper. I like that."

"Yes, young Samuel, you cut quite the dashing figure," Josh remarks in a haughty British accent.

Great. Even Josh gives better compliments than I do. And he's a freaking zombie.

Sam just laughs. "Thank you, Josiah."

So Josh's real name isn't *actually* Josiah. It's not even Joshua. It's just Josh. But see, everyone always assumes it's Joshua, so after having to insist over and over again that his name isn't Joshua, the guys all began calling him Josiah instead. I've actually seen fan websites that list his full name as Josiah Anthony Cahill. At first, it drove him crazy, but now he just throws his head back and laughs with the rest of us.

The only one who doesn't seem to be enjoying the evening all that much is Cory. Apparently, things got really tense after Sam and I left last night. If there's anything I can say for the boys of The Kind of September, it's that they look out for one another. They're all fiercely loyal and they always band together. I know that the others didn't like the way that Tara was talking to Sam, but they also didn't want to make it seem like they were ganging up on Cory or his new girlfriend. Needless to say, Tara isn't here tonight, but as far as I know, she's still in the picture.

The good news is I don't think Cory will stay mad for long. Performing alone will be enough to lift his spirits. Besides, I've never known any of the guys to hold a grudge for very long. I know Sam's already forgotten about last night. I'm sure the other guys have too. And even if he is still upset, he's going to have to at least pretend he's over it before they get up in front of the crowd.

As those in the business always say, the show must go on.

Chapter Nine

"She knows exactly what she wants
She don't take time to pretend
She knows that all the things you do
Won't make a difference in the end
She knows exactly what she needs
And it don't matter what you say
If you find another girl like her
Don't let her get away..."

Song: "Girls Like Her"
Artist: The Kind of September
From the Album: *The Kind of September*

The new album is coming out in less than a week. Singles have been released. The "This Is Real" music video has been released and has already been viewed by millions of fans online. The guys are in the process of filming a new video for their next single, "Meet Me on the Midway," which also happens to be the name of the new album. We've been shooting at Coney Island, which, let me tell you, might be the most fun thing I've ever done in my entire life. The guys are having the time of their lives filming in such an awesome setting.

Well, Jesse was a little antsy about riding the Wonder Wheel. He's fine with flying and being in tall hotel buildings, but Ferris wheels and other rides make him really fidgety and nauseous. What's worse is that, because he was so nervous, he had to keep re-shooting the very scenes that scared him. He ended up riding the Wonder Wheel a good four or five times more than his bandmates.

The good news is that he never actually puked. He did have to sit down for a while though after one particularly excruciating take on the roller coaster. If he looks a little green around the gills when the video is released, you'll know why.

Other than that slight setback and a few girls who were not extras slipping past security and onto the set, today went incredibly smoothly. There's still a lot of work to be done, but I think this video is going to be even better than the "This Is Real" video.

For now, however, we're all sitting back, relaxing and celebrating Cory and Joni's twenty-first birthday. Unfortunately for them, only Oliver is actually old enough to legally drink with them, so we're not going out. We have, however, had a feast brought in of pizza (yes, we eat a lot of pizza), ice cream, and an enormous birthday cake. Stan also surprised each of them with baskets full of booze, so even though the rest of us are underage, they still get their Congratulations-on-Being-Able-to-Legally-Drink drinks.

When it comes to presents, none of us ever really give anything too extravagant. For example, this year, I got Joni a gift card to her favorite coffee shop and a boatload of I ♥ NY paraphernalia to add to her collection and I got Cory a really nice set of vintage classic rock records. I've got to tell you, it's kind of tricky buying presents for friends who are filthy stinking rich, but the good thing about the guys is that they rarely splurge on everyday items like records. Cars and houses? Yes. But I'm not going to buy any of them a car or a house for their birthday, so it all works out.

Oliver's gift to Joni, however, is a little overwhelming. He went out and bought her a beautiful topaz birthstone necklace from Tiffany's. I have no idea how Joni hasn't figured out that he likes her by now. Want to know what Oliver got me for my last birthday? Socks. Granted, he bought them in England which, you know, was really nice of him. But come on.

Even Tara's gift to Cory didn't measure up to Oliver's incredible topaz necklace. Yes, Tara is here. Fortunately, she seems to be on her best behavior. True, she and Sam are totally ignoring each other, but if I'm being honest, I prefer it when beautiful girls who are also evil ignore him. And vice versa.

In case you're wondering, Tara got Cory and a gift receipt for a couple's spa day and a framed photo of her in a bikini. She didn't get Joni anything. I'm pretty sure the rest of us are silently judging her and thinking she's a horrible, horrible person, which she is. Interestingly enough, Oliver is the only one willing to give Tara the benefit of the doubt. I'm telling you, he's too nice for his own good.

"Maybe she doesn't realize that Joni and Cory are twins," Oliver reasons with me. Since the cake has been served, we've all split off into tiny groups. Sam and Josh are across the room laughing their heads off about something while Jesse is chatting with Tara and Cory, and Joni is out on the balcony with Stan and a few of the other managers. This finally leaves me with a few minutes to talk with Oliver.

"She's dating the guy. Surely it's come up."

"She also gets the two of you mixed up on a regular basis."

"True. Maybe she thinks we're twins," I remark. Oliver chuckles. I've never been very good at small talk, so I just come out and say it. "You like Joni, don't you?"

Oliver looks at me like some kind of strange, terrified, tattooed bird.

"No," he answers automatically. I raise an eyebrow. He sighs. "I don't know. Maybe. Not that it matters either way. She's made it quite clear that she's not interested in any of us."

"Well, maybe she would be if she knew how you felt about her."

"Come on, Mel, you know her. It's not just us. She's not interested in dating at all, and I don't want to force her into anything that she's not ready for. I'm not sure if that really makes any sense."

"No, it does," I told him honestly. "It makes perfect sense."

He looks at me. "Is that why you haven't told Sam how *you* feel?"

Now it's my turn to give him the bewildered animal facing their death look. As it turns out, that's not just an expression. I actually feel like a bewildered animal facing her death.

I laugh nervously. "You think I like Sam?"

"You mean you don't?"

"Well... I... Um..." I have so many questions bouncing around in my head right now that I can't quite remember how to make words. Why does he think that? Is it that obvious? Does everybody else know? Does Sam know? Did he ask Oliver to mention it to me? Does Oliver know about the talk Sam and I had that night that Tara came by the hotel and Sam and I slipped out to watch zombie movies?

Oh, God. I can't handle this. I really can't.

But Oliver, bless that kid, he seems to know exactly what I'm thinking.

"It's okay. No one else knows. I mean, I think we all suspect there's something. But nothing has been said."

"Okay good," I finally breathe.

I can't believe we're having this conversation. Furthermore, I can't believe we're having it while *Sam is actually in the room*. Fortunately, he and Josh are still in hysterics over something. Those two are hilarious together, and no one on Earth thinks they're funnier than they do.

"You two are so close. I can't believe you haven't told him yet." Oliver says.

"I - I just don't want to scare him off, you know? I don't want to pressure him into anything or make him feel like I'm expecting something from him. He doesn't need that."

"I know how you feel," Oliver says, gazing out the window at Joni.

"Hey!" Sam's loud voice makes both of us jump. He and Josh are strolling our way across the room. "Why are you two lurking in the corner over here?"

"We're plotting," I tell him, all the while secretly praying he didn't hear a word that Josh and I just said.

"What are you plotting?" Sam asks.

"Your downfall."

"As usual."

"Planning to stab me in the brain, Mel?" Josh asks. I knew I shouldn't have told him about that stupid zombie dream, because now he's never going to let me forget it. "I always knew you had it out for me."

"What gave me away?"

"Mostly the way you look at me like the Evil Queen looks at Snow White. Like you want my heart in a box." Josh grabs his chest like he's having a heart attack.

"Just so we're on the same page, you're Snow White in this scenario?" I ask.

"That's right," Josh announces, slinging his arm around Sam's shoulders. "And Sam here is my Dopey."

"I thought I was Doc," Sam says, looking far too disappointed.

"Bro, you are in no way smart enough to be Doc."

In case you were wondering, that kind of logic is precisely why Josh wins pretty much every debate or argument that happens to arise.

"So what are they discussing out there?" Sam asks, glancing out the window at the group on the balcony.

"I don't know," Oliver replies.

"Let's go find out," Josh says and barges outside, letting in a rush of frigid wind.

I consider sprinting back to my room for my coat (all I'm wearing right now are jeans and my favorite beige sweater, which is pretty but doesn't exactly keep me warm) but then I remember that if I look cold enough, then there's a chance that Sam will notice and wrap his arms around me.

It turns out that the people out on the balcony, also known as the managers, are having a conversation that is so boring, it shouldn't be allowed on a festive night in a city like this one. New York nights deserve talk of music and lights and everything that makes life extraordinary.

Sam gets it.

"You know, sometimes I still can't believe that we're here," he says to me, leaning against the rail and gazing out at the city, so beautiful that it almost doesn't seem real. The glow of the city lights illuminates his handsome face, and the brisk, cold breeze toys with his hair. Here, in this moment, he looks more like a star in a music video than he ever has on screen. To me, anyway. "It's been two years, and I'm still not completely used to it all."

I don't have to ask what "it" is.

"I'm not sure it's something that you ever fully get used to," I tell him. "It's still overwhelming to me and I'm not even in the band."

"You're still part of the group," he reminds me. "I bet if you actually made your Twitter account public, you'd have a million followers like that." He snaps his fingers.

"Maybe." I doubt it. But then, Joni is up to well over a million. Of course, interacting with fans is part of her job. "I don't know. I'm kind of happy being invisible."

"You're *not* invisible."

"Not completely, but I can still go out and enjoy a drink at Starbucks without being recognized." And I'm not complaining about that at all. In fact, I love it.

"True. I have to admit, I kind of envy you that," Sam tells me.

"You could go out in disguise," I suggest.

"You mean like with a fake mustache and a trench coat?" he laughs.

"You could try to grow a real mustache."

I say try because Sam, God bless him, is one of those guys who just can't grow facial hair. He's tried. Last year, all the guys decided to participate in No-Shave-November (about which all of us girls had very mixed feelings) and everyone was convinced Sam was cheating because he barely grew anything. Just a little sparse stubble on his chin and on his upper lip. It doesn't make him any less sexy, but the guys do like to give him a hard time about it every now and then. Especially Jesse, who, in thirty short days, grew one of the most extravagant and full, ginger-colored beards the world has ever seen.

"I think by the time I actually manage to grow a mustache, scientists will have invented a teleportation device that will enable me to phase in and out of public at my leisure thus eliminating any need I may have had for a disguise in the first place," Sam remarks.

What can I say? The man makes a valid argument.

"Well, at least you have a cute face," I tell him absently. It's nothing I haven't told him before, and certainly nothing he isn't already fully aware of. But it is the first time I've said something like that since confessing out loud that I'm actually in love with him and for some reason, I'm convinced that Oliver is somehow sending Sam telepathic messages about my feelings for him and I'm not going to lie to you, I'm kind of freaking out a little.

See, this is the kind of crazy that a guy like Sam really just doesn't need in his life.

Thankfully, he just grins at me. Sam never overreacts. He stays calm, cool, and collected. And confident. My gosh, he is so confident. Everything just comes so easily and naturally to him. That's something I've always loved about him, and something I've always envied. I also think it's why we work so well together as friends.

Of course, I'm hoping it means that we'll work even better together as something more.

Chapter Ten

"This time we have
The time we make
This time I love
The time we take
I'll never ever
Want this moment
In this time to end
So let's take some time
Take some time
Take some time to
Begin again."

Song: "Time"
Artist: The Kind of September
From the Album: *Meet Me on the Midway*

This morning when I open my eyes, everything is perfectly normal. The sun is shining through the white curtains of our hotel room, and Joni is drying her hair in the bathroom. Sam is lying next to me, smiling with what I can only call absolute delight and giddiness.

Oh wait, that's not normal.

"What the - ?" I croak, half-leaping, half-falling out of bed.

"Good morning, sunshine," he greets me with a cheeky grin.

"Did I *miss* something?" I demand.

"Incidentally, that's what I came to ask you."

"What are you talking about? And how did you get in here?"

"Joni let me in. But I'm afraid we have more pressing issues to discuss." And with that, he holds up his phone. His Twitter app is open to a list of Trending Topics. "Notice anything?"

Right off the bat? No, I don't. There's something about football, something about Kelli Barnett and her new nose job, something about outer space…

"Please don't tell me they found aliens."

"Unfortunately, not yet. Never give up hope, though."

"Okay, what am I looking at, then?" Sam grins points to a hashtag that I assumed was referring to something dumb that a celebrity or politician said. #*Meliver*. "What is me-liver?"

"Not me-liver. Mel-iver."

"And what does that - oh, God."

I know *exactly* what it means. I've learned that sometimes in the world of pop culture, fans like to make up what they like to call "ships." When you "ship" someone with another person, it means that you want those two people to be together romantically. For example, I totally ship myself and Sam Morneau.

When these ships come into existence, some fans take it upon themselves to create ship-names. These names usually come about by combining the couple's names. For example, Cory and Tara are Tary. Sam and I might be something like Samel or maybe Melissam.

And Oliver and I would be Meliver.

People all over the world think that Oliver and I are dating. There are even pictures of us looking really intimate in the corner last night to support this newly bred gossip.

That's it. My life is over.

"How did this happen?" I ask, my voice about ten times higher than usual.

"Take a wild guess," Sam remarks.

Of course. Why did I even have to ask? The only person who could possibly have posted these pictures, the only one seeking attention, the only one who doesn't know any of us well enough to know that we just don't *do* this kind of thing to one another is Tara.

"What did she say?"

"She posted the pictures on all of her social media accounts with the caption, *Hot new couple alert.*"

"Why would she do this? What is she trying to accomplish? And *why do you think this is so funny?*" I demand because Sam will not stop giggling. Seriously, I have never seen him this tickled.

"Because... this isn't necessarily a bad thing," he says.

"What, are you insane? Yes, this is a bad thing! This is a very bad thing!"

"No it's not. You know why? Because this isn't a big deal. Most people know Tara's the one who started which means they're not going to believe it."

Okay, that's a little bit true, but a lot of people totally believe it. Surprisingly enough, however, a lot of people seem sort of okay with it.

OMG Mel and Oliver are so cute! #Meliver4Ever

Mel seems so down to earth. I hope she and Oliver are happy together.

Oliver is dating Mel Parker? I never pictured them together, but now that they are, I think they're so perfect! #Meliver

Some are actually defending us, which would be really awesome, you know, if we were actually a couple.

Look TKOS personal lives are just that... PERSONAL. #MindYourOwnBusiness

Mel is a good friend of #TKOS and if she makes Oliver happy, then that's all that matters.

On the flip side, others are getting a bit defensive, and even a little threatening.

Guys... this is just a RUMOR. Oliver recently said in an interview that he is SINGLE.

I don't think I believe this #Meliver stuff. Melissa Parker is their friend. I really don't think she's romantically into any of them.

Then there are the ones who speak the truth. The ones who, like Sam said, seem to see right through Tara's twisted intentions.

I can't believe anyone believes in #Meliver. Tara Meeks is the one who tweeted it! #AttentionSeeker

Yeah, sure, Oliver is dating Mel Parker. If Tara Meeks told you that pigs could fly, would you believe her then?

Then there are the ones, particularly the girls who are hoping to one day be Mrs. Oliver Berkley, that are taking the non-news a bit harder.

Oliver NOOOO! You were supposed to wait for me! #Heartbroken

What?! Oliver has a girlfriend?! This can't be happening!

Oliver is taken. I have nothing more to live for. #Meliver #ForeverAlone

Those are the ones I feel really sorry for. I feel like I stole one of the most important people in their lives from them. And I'm not even dating him! I wish I could tweet each of those girls individually to assure them I did not steal their man.

Although technically, he is kind of into someone else, but they don't need to know that!

"It's also not a bad thing," Sam continues, "because so far, no one from the media is harassing you about it. No one is saying anything bad about you. I'd like to think that means that if one of us were to date someone that people actually like, then maybe all the rumors and tabloids would go away."

"Sam, you know I love you, but I think that might be a bit of a stretch," I tell him. Yes, I tell him I love him, but as a friend, of course. I'd never tell him how much I *really* love him.

"Hey, I'm always betting on the long shots," he reminds me as a freshly groomed Joni emerges from the bathroom.

"Mel, I heard your squeaky voice. What's wrong?" File that comment under Signs-You-Might-Have-Lived-With-The-Same-People-for-too-Long.

"Tara started a rumor that she and Oliver are dating," Sam answers for me.

"She *what*?!" Joni demands. At first I wonder if maybe she's jealous and that she really does like Oliver after all and she's just been really good at hiding it. Then I remember that Joni is the most uptight, anal-retentive person alive and that she really hates Tara Meeks.

"If it makes you feel better, a lot of people think we're cute," I tell her, feeling a little defeated myself. I'm hoping Sam is right, and it's something that will pass very, very quickly.

"That's it. I've had it with her. I'm going to talk to Cory," Joni announces, grabbing her massive bag full of Lord Knows What that she carries with her everywhere she goes.

"He's not here," Sam says.

"What do you mean he's not here?"

"Let's see... how do I put this delicately? I was absent a roommate last night. I went to bed alone and woke up alone. Your brother spent the night shacked up in a different hotel with his girlfriend."

"That was very delicate," I tell him.

Joni, on the other hand, throws Sam such a venomous look that he actually recoils a little. In fact, he even looks kind of remorseful.

"Sorry," he apologizes. "Look, I know you don't like her, but it's not like Cory is a bad guy or just doing this to upset you. He really likes her. I honestly don't get it, but I know Cory. He's smart and responsible and he's got a good head on his shoulders. And come on, he's not the first guy to go a bit stupid over a girl. It happens to the best of us."

"We've noticed," Joni narrows her eyes. She's a little less sympathetic to the constant rumors of Sam's womanizing and hard-partying than the rest of us are. Then, she relaxes a bit. "I'm sorry," she says, sinking down onto the foot of my bed. "That was uncalled for. I know I'm overreacting. I just... I *hate* seeing my brother being used like this. I'd hate it for any of you with a leech like Tara, but I especially hate it for him. I'm supposed to take care of him, you know?"

"I know," I tell her. "But the thing is, Cory is a grown man. As weird as it is for me to say that about a guy who, not three months ago, was bragging about his new Batman underwear - "

"Hey! Don't be hating on the Batman briefs," Sam interrupts.

For once, I choose to ignore him. "The point is I know you feel protective of him, but he's going to make his own decisions, and whatever happens is not your responsibility."

"Well, actually, as one of our managers, it kind of is," Sam butts in again.

"Sam, has anyone ever told you that you are exceedingly unhelpful?" Joni asks. Then she turns to me. "What about you?"

"What about me?" I ask.

"Mel, you're one of my best friends in the world. I don't want to see her hurting you like this either," she tells me.

Aw. I kind of want to reach out and hug her, but I know Joni really isn't a fan of being touched. Still, she exposes her soft side so infrequently that I can't help but feel a little loved.

"Thank you, Joni. I'm okay. But I appreciate it," I say. Then I wonder, "What does Oliver think about all this?"

"I don't know. Haven't talked to him," Sam mutters, stretching back onto the bed and resting his head against my pillows.

"No, no, don't do that." Joni scolds him.

"What?" he asks.

"You have a music video to shoot. No going back to sleep. Up."

"Ugh" Sam groans. But he's back up, with a smile on his face. He loves shooting music videos, and I know he's especially excited to get back to Coney Island. I say this with absolutely no bias, I think this will be one of their best music videos yet.

That is, if we can keep the drama to a minimum.

Cory is already waiting when the rest of us arrive on set.

"Good morning, amigos," he greets us. He's in a really good mood.

That's probably a bad thing.

The guys greet him like there isn't an enormous metaphorical elephant stomping around Coney Island, but Joni cuts right to the chase.

"So Cory, have you checked Twitter recently?" she asks as the rest of the guys disperse. I hang back with Joni just in case she needs any moral support. I also really want to eavesdrop on their Tara conversation.

"Actually, Sis, I haven't. Why, did Sam get another girl pregnant?"

Okay, that joke is not funny. Last year, some girl from Tacoma, Washington, whom Sam has never even met, not only claimed that he was the father of her unborn baby, but actually filed a lawsuit requesting he take a paternity test. It was ridiculous. Now of course, nothing came of it, but it was still a huge mess.

But Joni is in no mood for her brother's odd sense of humor. "Your girlfriend told the entire Internet that Oliver is dating Mel."

"What?" Cory asks. Then he looks at me. "You and Oliver are dating?"

"No, nimrod! That's the point!" Joni snaps. "Tara is starting up rumors about your friends and bandmates. What do you think about that, Romeo?"

"Well, first of all, I think you need to take a chill pill. And second, I'm sure it's all just a big misunderstanding."

"Did you actually just use the phrase take a chill pill?" I ask. Seriously, I haven't heard anyone use that in a real conversation since I was about nine.

Both Foreman twins stare at me like someone who totally and completely missed the point, which, you know, is kind of fair. But Joni is back to business soon enough.

"Cory, you don't get it. This is your career. There isn't even room for little misunderstandings, let alone big ones."

"Okay, okay, fine. I'll have a talk with her," Cory agrees.

"No, I don't think that's a good idea. This girl has got you blinded. She's stirring up unnecessary drama behind your back and you don't even realize it."

"You know, Joni, you have been bitter and cynical about this relationship since day one. And you know why I think that is? I think you're jealous."

"*Excuse me*?" Joni demands. It's a good thing looks can't actually kill, because Cory would be flat-lining right now.

"Yeah. You don't like it that I'm with someone and you're not. But you know what? You've brought that upon yourself."

"And what does *that* mean?"

"You know exactly what it means. You could have guys lining up to date you if you would just give them a chance, but no. You're still too hung up on Jesse to open yourself up to someone new."

I actually laugh at that. Aside from me dating Oliver and Sam knocking up some weird girl from Tacoma, Joni still being hung up on Jesse is the most ridiculous thing I've ever heard.

That is, until I see the look on Joni's face. She looks exposed, vulnerable, and, to my utter shock, on the verge of tears.

"You know what, Cory? You can go to hell," she hisses.

And with that, she turns and flees the scene.

Chapter Eleven

"Won't you take me back
To that summer sunset
And the way you looked at
The fire in the sky
And won't you take me back
To that beginning of forever
Please tell me you remember
Us together..."

Song: "Fire in the Sky"
Artist: The Kind of September
From the Album: *The Kind of September*

I feel terrible.

Joni is still heartbroken over Jesse. Have I really been so blinded and preoccupied with my own hopeless pining over Sam that I didn't notice what she was going through? What kind of friend am I, anyway?

A terrible one, that's what.

I mean, I know that she changed a bit after Jesse broke up with her. She doesn't open up as often as she used to. She also doesn't laugh as much as she used to. She's a lot more guarded now. Maybe that was intentional. Maybe she didn't want any of us to know how much the breakup with Jesse actually affected her, and that's why she became so strict and serious. Or maybe it's a type of defense mechanism. If she doesn't let anyone in, then she won't get hurt again.

There's only one way to find out for sure.

I find her sitting by herself next to the carousel, which the guys will be filming on sometime later today. She's going over notes on her iPad, but she seems distracted. She's so lost in thought, in fact, that she doesn't even notice me until I call her name.

She looks up, clearly startled. When she realizes it's only me, she looks relieved, but still slightly embarrassed. "Oh, hey," she greets me. "Just going over the schedule for the day."

"Are you okay?" I ask her.

"Oh yeah, I'm fine. I'm still a little pissed off about those stupid rumors, but I don't want it to get in the way of shooting today."

"I meant about Jes - "

But Joni holds up a hand and cuts me off.

"Mel. You know what? I'm just going to stop you there. I have absolutely no feelings for Jesse Scott. Cory is an idiot if he thinks I do."

"Are you sure? It would be understandable if you did. I mean, he was your first real boyfriend."

"No, he was a guy I dated briefly in high school. My first real relationship is going to be mature. And thoughtful. And not with some pretty, egotistical pop-rocker."

I think of Oliver and have to bite my tongue. I'm usually pretty good at keeping secrets, but I'd also like to think that Joni might feel differently if she knew about his feelings for her. Somehow, I'm able to fight the desire to spill everything that Oliver told me the night before. But just barely.

"That might be the case," I say, taking a seat next to her, "but it still could have hurt your feelings, you know, when it ended."

"Mel... Come on. You know I don't like talking about stuff like this."

"I know. But sometimes you need to talk about it. Otherwise you carry it all inside and it just sits there, taking up space in your mind that could be used for more important things." Like the cute British guy who is head over heels for her.

Joni looks at me and the corner of her mouth lifts into a half-smile. "You should be a therapist."

"I'd love that. I could get paid to talk," I smile. The truth is I would make a terrible therapist. I'm far too obsessive, analytical, and, let's be honest here, neurotic to ever qualify for a job in the mental health industry.

"You should start with Cory," Joni quips.

"Unfortunately, I think infatuation is the most socially acceptable form of insanity," I tell her. "It's also probably the most common."

"Yeah," she says shortly. Then she stares back down at her tablet.

"So... Do you want to talk about it?" I ask.

She looks back at me, her eyes softer and somehow lighter than usual. It's not hard to see why Oliver has a crush on her. She really is beautiful, with brown hair that falls in soft curls around her face, even when most of it is clipped up, and big green eyes that give her a look of innocence, kind of like a Disney Princess.

The thing is, she doesn't want people to see her as beautiful or innocent or any of that. She wants to be admired for her intelligence, her drive, and her accomplishments, not her looks. She was like that even before she started dating Jesse. It's something I've always respected and admired about her.

But I'd be lying if I said it doesn't make my day every time a guy tells me he thinks I'm pretty.

Finally, Joni sighs. "I'm not still hung up on Jesse. At least, not in the way Cory thinks. I don't want him back. I'm not secretly longing for him to come ravish me in the middle of the night. I just... I want to be okay with him. And I'm *not*.

And I don't, for one second, want him to think that he messed me up so badly that I'm afraid to open up or share my feelings with anyone on the off chance that he'll figure it out. And I can't give him that kind of satisfaction. I just can't."

"Joni, I don't think Jesse is proud of what he did to you," I tell her. "I think he respects you and I think he really is sorry that he hurt you. He just wasn't ready for a commitment, you know? Like you said, it wasn't like you two were engaged or in a long-term serious relationship. You just dated in high school. Most high school relationships don't last."

"I know," she says. "And you're right. I know he felt bad about it. I've just had a hard time forgiving him."

"That's okay. I still haven't forgiven Sam for telling me that we all have microscopic mites living on our eyelashes."

"That's gross."

"I know, right? He told me that in eighth grade and it still gives me nightmares."

Joni smiles at me. "Thank you."

"What for?" I ask.

"For being a good friend." Then, she gathers up her iPad and her bag and stands up. "Come on. Let's go shoot a music video."

❁♫♩❊

I don't actually get a chance to talk to Oliver about our newfound relationship until we break for lunch. Even then, it's not much of a real conversation because we're surrounded by his bandmates who all find the situation totally hilarious. Josh, especially.

"I wish you two had told us you wanted to be alone. We would have reserved you your own private room," he snickers.

"Oh will you please *shut it*?" Oliver snaps. Thankfully, he's just as unamused as I was earlier this morning.

"Hey, maybe Mel could star in our next music video. We could put her on a balcony and have Oliver sing to her," Jesse grins, getting in on the action. Sometimes, he tries so hard to be funny. He's just not.

"Or maybe we could have them on an ocean liner, holding each other and looking out over the waves!" Josh adds.

"I kind of want to see them pull off the move from *Dirty Dancing*," Sam grins.

"I hate you all," I mutter, taking a swig of soda. I'm just glad that neither Cory nor Joni is here for this conversation. I'm not sure where they are, but I'm hoping they're talking things out.

"I do, too," Oliver agrees with me.

"Aw, see? You're so perfect together," Josh laughs and draws a stupid heart in the air with his fingers.

"Josh, I'm warning you," I threaten, but of course, I've got nothing. I'm not devious or quick enough to actually come up with anything good. Besides, Josh knows no boundaries. Once, in high school, he set three chickens loose in the courtyard. They were all wearing signs that read *#1, #3,* and *#4.* I cannot tell you how long the faculty and staff spent searching for chicken *#2* before they figured out that it didn't exist.

You see, that is why all threats I make toward Josh Cahill are totally and completely empty. I fear retaliation, especially from him.

"Don't worry, Mel. I've already sent out a tweet explaining that this is all just a false rumor," Oliver assures me.

"Aw, why?" Josh asks.

"Josh, are you becoming a fangirl?" I ask.

"No. It was kind of entertaining though, reading all the different opinions on it. And seeing how twitchy it makes the two of you."

"You're a terrible human being," Oliver says.

"But I'm so cute!" Josh protests. "Just the other day, a fan tweeted that she wanted to cuddle up with me by a fire in matching onesie pajamas. If that isn't adorable, I don't know what is."

"I'd actually pay money to see you in a onesie," Sam remarks.

"So, are people actually responding to what you said?" I ask Oliver.

"Most are. Some are disappointed. Some are convinced that we're just not ready to go public yet. But honestly, I don't think anyone's really surprised, you know, considering the source," Oliver replies.

"You mean Tara?" Jesse asks through a mouthful of turkey sandwich.

"Yeah," I say.

"This year for Christmas, I'm getting all of us matching onesies," Josh announces. This results in a group-stare from Jesse, Oliver, Sam, and me. I honestly have no idea what exists in that massive space in between Josh's ears, but I'm fairly certain it's not a functioning human brain.

"What the heck is wrong with you?" Oliver asks.

"Where do I begin, brother?" Josh asks and downs the last of his bottled water. Josh doesn't drink soda. He says that the carbonation makes his tongue hurt. And yet, he has about twenty tattoos. Don't those make your skin hurt?

Josh is a strange bird.

By now, our lunch break is just about over so we clear our trash away and prepare for the final stretch of shooting. We got all of the sunset and nighttime shots filmed yesterday, so the guys just need to finish up the daytime bits (which are, incidentally, for the first half of the video), and it will be a wrap.

I'm not filming, today. Instead, I'm taking photographs of the guys and the set for their website, publicity, social media, what have you.

As I'm checking the camera to make sure I have the proper batteries, memory cards, and lenses, I hear a high-pitched squeal somewhere off to my right. I glance up and am horrified to see Cory, spinning a delighted Tara Meeks around in his arms. She's laughing and shrieking about something that will probably ruin my day, but I try to ignore her and go back to my equipment check.

It's rather difficult to ignore someone, however, when they're suddenly hovering over your shoulder.

"Melinda, hi," she greets me. Well, at least Melinda is closer to Melissa than Meredith or Joni. We are making progress, it seems. "Listen, Cory told me that you were a little upset this morning about what I tweeted and I just wanted you to know that I'm sorry. I didn't mean to step on any toes."

Usually, I'm the kind of person who shrugs things off without much fuss. No harm done. Water under the bridge. Oh, I know you didn't mean any harm. That sort of thing.

So it's pretty uncharacteristic of me to respond with, "Tara, you didn't step on my toes. You told a flat out lie about me. To the entire world."

Her big, mascaraed eyes widen. This was clearly not the reply she was expecting.

"That's a little harsh, don't you think? I mean, what was I supposed to think? You and Oliver looked awfully cozy last night, huddled together in that corner."

"You also saw me curled up in a blanket with Sam last week but I didn't see any Hot New Couple Alerts then," I remind her.

"Well, he's Sam. I mean, come on. If he wasn't interested in Courtney, he's definitely not going to be interested in you."

I don't know what's more offensive: the idea that I'm not good enough for Sam or what she seems to be insinuating about Oliver. What, Sam can afford to be picky but Oliver can't? Oliver has about a fifth of the world's young female population falling at his feet.

I swear, everything about this girl makes me want to slap her.

"Wow," I finally say. "You know, Tara, you are really something. Tell me, are you always this bitchy, or is it something you save for your boyfriend's coworkers?"

Oh my God.

What have I done? I've never said anything like that in my life! I'm supposed to be the nice one! The good girl who never gets in trouble! I don't pick fights! And I definitely don't stand up to Queen Bees like Tara Meeks. My mouth is doing that thing where it totally bypasses my brain and says whatever the heck it wants.

Oh, this is *so* not the time or place for this.

"What did you just say to me?" Tara hisses.

I'm not going to lie. I'm terrified. But somehow, I manage to stand my ground.

"Look, I don't know you, and you clearly don't care about knowing me or else you'd at least make a tiny effort to remember my name. But you seem really clueless to me, especially when it comes to treating Cory, his friends, and most importantly, his fans with respect."

Tara looks flabbergasted, if not utterly dumbfounded.

"I cannot believe I actually came over here to apologize to you," she sneers.

"Yeah, neither can I. Frankly, you weren't very good at that either."

What has gotten into me? I promise you, I am not this person! Something about her is just bringing out the absolute worst in me. I don't like it at all.

But I also don't really want to stop it.

Tara, meanwhile, is positively seething. She also seems to be calculating, trying to figure out a way to let me know that I've messed with the wrong model.

"I don't know who you think you are, but let me put things in perspective for you," she says, her blue eyes cool and narrow. "I'm dating one of the world's biggest stars. You clean up after him. I have thousands of fans and followers all over the world. You have a camera and a nose that's too long for your lopsided face. People recognize me as someone they want to be. Those same people don't even know that you exist. So if I were you, I'd keep those snarky comments and lousy attitude to myself, because you have no idea what I could do to you."

For those wondering, being threatened by a super model is a lot scarier than you'd think it'd be. But I'm not about to let her think she's won or succeeded in her efforts to belittle me.

However, before I can dig myself into an even deeper hole, Stan calls over that they're about to start shooting and that I need to get a move on. Even though I didn't get the last word in, I'm only too eager to get away and have nothing more to do with Tara Meeks.

I only hope that the feeling is mutual.

Chapter Twelve

"And she walks like winter across the room
And I can smell her sweet perfume
Snowlight dancing, frozen blue
Winter's dress looks good on you
The Northern Lights, they shine for you
This winter night was made for two..."

Song: "Snowlight"
Artist: The Kind of September
From the Album: *17 Times Over*

Tonight, I just want to be alone.

I've spent what should have been a fun and exciting afternoon wallowing in guilt over what I said to Tara.

No, not guilt. Guilt would imply that I care about how what I said may have affected her, and I'm a bit ashamed to admit that I don't. I guess that's what I'm feeling right now. Shame. I'm ashamed that I stooped to her level. I've never been that kind of person, you know? I don't say things like that, no matter how upset I am. But I'm so sick of her spreading rumors and I'm especially sick of everyone else acting like it's okay.

I haven't had the guts to face Cory. I'm sure Tara's told him everything that happened. I think Sam knows something is bothering me, but they were called in for a last-minute radio interview after filming wrapped, so I haven't gotten the chance to talk to him. Besides, he and the guys have got to be exhausted. They don't need to be dealing with drama, especially drama that I created.

That's what's bothering me the most. This is so unlike me! I don't stir up drama. Especially with people like Tara who specialize in it.

But what's done is done. Maybe I can apologize to Cory. That is, if he's still talking to me. I bet you anything Tara has gone crying to him, telling him how mean I am and how I deserve to be excommunicated.

To be honest, I've kind of enjoyed having a few hours all to myself. I took a long shower. I painted my toenails. I plucked my eyebrows. I basically treated myself to an at-home makeover. It was nice. So often on the road and behind the scenes, I don't pay much attention to what I wear or how I look.

Now I'm alone in Joni's and my hotel room, lounging on the bed and watching *Titanic*. True, it's not the best movie to watch when I'm already feeling a little sad, but at least it's quality. That's all that really matters.

About halfway through the movie, someone knocks on the door. It's probably Joni, though it's not like her to forget her key.

When I open the door, however, Joni isn't the one standing there. It's Sam.

"Hey," I greet him. It's funny. You'd think right about now, I'd be fighting an impulse to run to the bathroom to check my reflection and make sure I look alright, but I'm not lying to you when I say Sam and I have seen each other at our absolute worst. He stuck by me after my wisdom teeth extraction, and I camped out with him on his couch after he came down with a terrible case of food poisoning. The fact that I came out of that situation still totally infatuated is, quite frankly, a miracle. Seriously, if I saw any other guy puke into a trash can beside the sofa, I'd be gone like *that*.

Long story short, the only reason I'm blushing right now is because Sam showed up unexpectedly. Not because he caught me in my pajamas and post-shower hair.

Sure enough, he comments, "You look cozy."

"Yeah," I reply. "Just kind of having a relaxing evening. How was the interview?"

"It was fine. Just talked about the album. Had a few laughs."

"That's good," I say. I'm hesitant to ask Sam if Cory said anything about Tara, because I'm honestly not sure if I want to know the answer. But I also know that I probably won't be able to face Cory until I find out if he's upset. "So uh... Did Cory say anything? You know, about anything that may have happened this afternoon?"

"You mean the thing where you accused Tara of being a very non-family-friendly word, a liar, and an all-around horrible human being? Yeah, he may have mentioned it." He says, leaning casually against the doorframe.

"Is he mad at me?"

"Well, Tara definitely is. But you know Cory. He's on everybody's side. He told her he was certain you didn't mean it and said that you were just looking out for Oliver."

"God, he gives me way too much credit."

"Yeah, that's what I said." Sam remarks. I throw him a look. "Kidding! To tell you the truth, I'm kind of proud of you."

"Why?" I mean, I'm glad to hear it, but I don't understand it. I'm not proud of me.

"I think there's a time and a place for everything. I think you know when something needs to be said and when you need to keep your thoughts and opinions to yourself. And I think that something needed to be said to her. Maybe not *exactly* the words you used..." Sam does not like cursing. It's funny, because he is such a guy in so many ways, but unlike his bandmates, three of whom swear like sailors, he prefers nicer words. "But the overall gist, I think she needed to hear. I don't think she really sees any of us as real people."

"I don't think she does either."

And that brings any and all talk of Tara Meeks to a close. It's for the best. I'm sick of thinking about her.

"So, is this your big plan for the evening? Sit around and watch sad girl movies all by yourself?"

"Pretty much."

"That sounds like a terrible night. You know what you should do? Go with me to Josh's room for a game night."

"A game night?" I ask.

"Yeah. On our way back from the interview, a few fans approached us and gave Josh all these games, like Twister and Monopoly so he and Jesse and Oliver decided to host an impromptu game night. Now just try to convince me that that doesn't sound like more fun than watching what might actually be the most depressing movie in history."

I have to admit, he's got a point. Though *Titanic* is far from the most depressing movie in history.

"I don't think I can," I admit.

"Perfect. Let's go."

❀♫♪❀

Here's the thing about The Kind of September. If you hang out with them on a regular basis, there is a good chance you will end up in a photograph, a tweet, a TikTok, or a YouTube video. Sometimes, all of the above. It's not a bad thing. The guys really love their fans, and they want to share as much of their lives with them as possible without getting too personal.

That, and they just really love performing for the camera, even when that camera happens to be a smartphone.

The point is I am not at all surprised to find Jesse filming Josh, Joni, and Cory, engrossed in an intense game of Candy Land while Oliver giggles over their shoulders. If that wasn't funny enough, Josh is wearing a red Solo cup as a hat. I'm tempted to ask, but I'm actually pretty sure I don't want to know.

Sam, on the other hand, looks highly offended and asks, "What the heck is this? You're playing Candy Land without me?"

"Sorry, bro, we couldn't resist," Josh replies without tearing his eyes away from the board.

"If it makes you feel better, we haven't played Pretty, Pretty Princess yet," Jesse assures him, reaching up to twirl a lock of Sam's blond hair. Sam swats him away, but laughs nevertheless.

"Dibs on the pink jewelry," Josh announces. I can't tell whether he's kidding or not.

They actually have quite the impressive collection of games going. Operation, Boggle, Sorry, Clue, Twister, and Monopoly are all in a pile in the middle of the room.

"So, a fan just walked up to you and gave you all these games?" I ask.

"Yep," Josh replies.

"Why?"

"She said that I once tweeted that I got bored during long bus rides, so she just went out and bought all these game for us."

"Wow, how sweet of her."

I remember when the guys first started out, they didn't know how to feel about all the gifts that fans showered them with. Granted, some of them were pretty strange. For example, one girl gave Sam a T-shirt with a Photoshopped picture of the two of them getting married. I'm not kidding. Sam, though, was very gracious and did an excellent job of acting like he wasn't completely creeped out.

A lot of gifts are also wildly inappropriate. I don't really want to go into that, but every time one of the guys receives a gift or a tribute that crosses a line, they go out of their way to remind young girls to respect their bodies and themselves. That's probably something I love most about them. They really care about their fans and they don't want to see them degrading themselves or feeling pressured to look or dress or act a certain way.

For all of those reasons, and the fact that they're just good, old-fashioned fun, these board games are probably the best gift the guys have ever received.

"I hope you gave her something in return," Joni says to Josh.

"I gave her a hug," he says.

"Not an autograph? Or a free CD?" If possible, Joni is even more about fan appreciation than the guys are. But for the guys, it's because they genuinely appreciate the fans. With Joni, it's more about image. Right now, she's probably imagining headlines about how rude and unappreciative Josh Cahill is towards fans who give him gifts.

Josh, on the other hand, is unconcerned.

"She just said she wanted a hug."

I'll admit, Josh does give pretty good hugs. I feel like there are stereotypes in every boy band. If that is, in fact, the case, then Josh is definitely The Cute One. He knows it, too. He thinks he can get away with anything with a smile and a cuddle.

Unfortunately for us, he usually can.

"So, Mel, the interviewer today was pretty disappointed to hear that you and Oliver broke up," Jesse informs me.

Seriously? Do we have to keep bringing this up? Can't it just go away?

"Oh, for the love of - We were never even together!" I remind them.

"By the way, Mel, you should know that Tara really is sorry," Cory tells me. "Maybe the two of you could talk, sort this thing out."

Oh Cory. There are so many things I want to say to you right now. Beginning with "your girlfriend is an evil banshee" and ending with "you are so sweet but so naive to think that she actually cares about mending fences with me."

Instead of all that, I say, "Maybe we can."

I don't like having to lie to keep the peace, but I am glad that Cory isn't angry with me. He's one of my best friends. The guys are so busy and off with so many people in so many places at so many different times, that sometimes, it can be easy to forget how much they all really mean to me. That's why nights together like this are so important.

"Alright, I'm going to go set up Twister," Sam announces. "Who's in?"

"Me!" I exclaim. Twister with Sam? As if I'm going to pass up *that* opportunity.

"I'll play," Oliver agrees.

"I am going to whoop all of you so hard, you're going to have nightmares about it," Josh announces, thus effectively ending the game of Candy Land.

"This, I've got to see," Jesse announces, phone in hand and ready to record.

Within just a few turns, my right hand is on blue, my left foot is on green, and I'm quickly discovering that I'm not nearly as flexible as I was in my youth. Okay, I'm still pretty young, but twenty-year-olds are a lot less limber than most of the kids who play this game.

It does make me feel better, however, to see that Sam, Oliver, and Josh are, if possible, even less flexible than I am, which is kind of surprising considering how much dancing and jumping around the stage that they do.

"Ow, ow. There goes my back," Josh groans.

"I thought you were going to whoop us all," Sam reminds him with a rather pathetic grimace.

"I lied."

"I can't believe people actually enjoy this game," Oliver adds.

I can. It's because even though my arms are about to give out and I'm pretty sure I've pulled a muscle in my leg, my back is also pressed directly against Sam's lean, muscular torso and his right hand, also on blue, is next to mine. I'm glad I took the time to shower, because I can feel his breath on the back of my neck and behind my ear.

Jesse, meanwhile, is snapping pictures of us on his phone.

"You guys look ridiculous," he laughs.

"Please don't post those pictures," I beg.

"Don't worry, I won't. I wouldn't want to compromise your already tarnished reputation," he teases.

"Oh, shut up."

"Ow, ow, ow. Okay, I'm done. I give up," Josh announces and collapses right on top of Oliver's leg.

"Agh!" Oliver cries out, toppling into me and Sam. So much for Twister.

"Please be careful," Joni tells us. "The American Music Awards are in three days. I don't want to see any of you limping through your performance."

Oh, right. I totally forgot about the American Music Awards. The guys are up for two awards, including Artist of the Year, and they're performing one of their songs off of the new album. We're all flying to Los Angeles the day after tomorrow, and then the day after the awards, it's right back to New York for the *Meet Me on the Midway* release celebration, which will be taking place the next day.

It's going to be a busy week. Fun, but busy.

"You know who else is going to be there?" Jesse asks with a wicked grin. "Chloe Conley."

"I thought we agreed that we'd never mention that name again," Josh says loudly.

I've told you before that a group of guys can't be as cute and famous as The Kind of September without having to endure the Media Gossip Machine. Basically, if any of them are spotted with a girl, regardless of the circumstances, rumors are going to circulate that the two are dating. Well, last year, the Internet took rumors of Josh and a singerl named Chloe Conley to the next level. Supposedly, not only were they secretly dating, but he'd been sneaking around with her while he was still dating his former girlfriend. There were even rumors of her visiting his parents and potential elopement talks. All of that stemmed from one photograph of the pair dancing at one of the after-parties. It was *insane*. It wasn't until a few months later that Josh found out that her people had started the rumors in order to generate some publicity for her. Josh still hasn't gotten over it.

"You know what the worst part is?" Cory says. "Her music isn't even that good."

"Cory, I think that's the first time I've ever heard you say something that isn't nice about someone," Sam remarks.

"But it's true. Her voice is so whiny," Cory says.

"And Josh is the one who made her that way," Jesse laughs.

"I hate you, you know that? You're actually the worst," Josh says.

"Look on the positive side. You've only got one fake ex running around the awards show. Sam's got hundreds," Oliver reminds him.

"Lucky me," Sam sighs.

"Hey, play your cards right, and you might have another one before the night is over!" Jesse tells him.

And that's when Sam tackles him to the ground. Josh follows, and, I guess just for the heck of it, Cory jumps in too. The only man still standing is Oliver as the four of them wrestle around on the ground like kids on the playground.

"Someone is going to lose an eye," he remarks.

"Or at least a few teeth," I add.

"Seriously. It's like they don't listen to me at all," Joni huffs and crosses her arms across her chest.

I've said it before and I'll say it again. There is never a dull moment.

Chapter Thirteen

"I'm running out of words to say
And I don't want to keep you waiting
Time is flying, baby, yes I know
But your eyes have got me hesitating
Can I tell you that I love you?
Tell you that I need you?
Tell you that I'm never, ever, ever
Gonna let you go?
Can I tell you that I want you?
And I need to be beside you?
Can I tell you, because I want you to know
I'll never let you go."

Song: "Tell You"
Artist: The Kind of September
From the Album: *17 Times Over*

It's the night of the American Music Awards in Los Angeles, and I've just realized something:

Both of my final exams for my online classes are this week and I haven't studied for them. At all. Seriously, why did I think that taking college classes and working a full-time job with a popular boy band would be a good idea?

Oh yeah. I wanted to make my parents proud. How overrated is that?

The good news is that since these exams are taken online, they're both open-note and open-book. However, they're also timed, so it's not like I can sit around and look every answer up and still expect to finish. Maybe I can sneak a textbook into the awards tonight. Right now, I'm reviewing notes on my laptop, but I'm not really absorbing anything.

Sam doesn't understand why I'm stressed out. Actually, he doesn't understand why I'm taking classes at all.

"You do know you're pretty much set for life, right?" he asks me. He's already dressed for the red carpet and let me tell you, he looks amazing. He's in black slacks, a white shirt, and a black vest. Seriously, what is it about guys in vests?

"No. *You're* set for life. I still might need something to fall back on," I remind him.

"Hey, as long as we're set for life, you're set for life. Unless you do something crazy, like rob a bank or kill a person."

"Oh, darn. You just ruined all my holiday plans," I joke.

"In all seriousness, though. Do you actually enjoy taking these classes? Or are you just doing it because you think it's what you're supposed to be doing?"

"A little of both," I admit. "You know, when I first started taking them, we really didn't know where all this was going. I thought I needed a backup plan."

It's true. None of us had any idea how big The Kind of September would get, not even its members. Even when they were writing music and holding auditions and performing locally in the Bay Area, none of them imagined one day being invited to perform for the American Music Awards, let alone being nominated for Artist of the Year. I think the most they ever hoped for was an indie record and enough support to travel around the country. No one dared to dream they'd be here in only a few short years.

"I get that," Sam tells me. "Still, you shouldn't stress out over it. It's not like a B in a few online classes is going to completely derail your life."

"I know. But I don't want all the work I've done this semester to have been for nothing."

"You're a real nerd, you know that?" Sam asks, flopping back onto my bed.

"And you're going to get in trouble with Tiffany if you mess up your hair. And when that happens, I am going to laugh."

"Touché." But Sam doesn't move. "You are happy, aren't you?"

That surprises me. I turn away from my computer screen to look at him.

"Of course I am. Why wouldn't you think so?"

"I don't know. With all the rumors and drama and now the additional school stuff... I just want to make sure you're still happy."

"I am," I assure him. "I actually can't imagine life getting any better."

"You kind of say that like it's a bad thing."

Do I? I don't hear it. But Sam is usually pretty good at knowing what's going on inside my head, apart from the whole being in love with him thing.

"It's not a bad thing. It's kind of a scary thing, but not necessarily bad."

"Why is it scary?"

It really doesn't make sense when you hear it out loud, but I'm not sure I know how to explain it.

"I guess I feel like when life is so good, there's a lot more to lose. And that worries me," I tell him.

At that, Sam sits back up and looks at me.

"You think you're going to lose us? Why would you think that?"

"I don't. I just... Ugh, I don't know! Now you've got me thinking and worrying that you don't think I'm happy and I promise you, I am!"

"Okay, okay, I'm sorry," Sam laughs. "The last thing I want is to make you *think*."

"Thank you!" Now I'm laughing, too. Unfortunately, though, I'm still thinking.

I'd never admit it to Sam, but I do worry about the future, because as much as I'd like it to, I don't think this will last forever. One day, The Kind of September won't be together anymore. They might do reunion tours, but eventually, they'll all go their separate ways. Most bands do. But even if they don't break up, we'll all get older and the guys will meet new people and eventually, Sam will fall in love with someone for real. That's the day I'm really dreading, because I can see that happening sooner than the band breaking up. And as much as I hate the idea of letting my feelings for a guy interfere with my life and career, I truly don't know if I'll be able to handle it when that day comes.

This is why you should never fall in love with your best friend. Or your coworkers. It can get really complicated and really depressing. And I don't want it to be depressing! Tonight, we're going to the American Music Awards! True, I won't be able to sit with them or anything, since they'll be up front and performing, but it's still an incredibly cool and exciting thing! Maybe, with any luck, I'll run into that hot Irish guy again and he won't remember me. He doesn't know it, but if Sam ends up falling in love with someone else, he's my real backup plan.

Hey, a girl can dream.

❀♫♪❀

Growing up, I was taught that the difference between being an extrovert and being an introvert was that extroverts are loud and outgoing and like to talk and introverts are quiet and shy and prefer to listen. I never knew exactly what I was, since when I'm around my friends, I can be as loud and outgoing as they are and yet, in big crowds or surrounded by strangers, I often find myself mute.

It wasn't until I took an online personality test (that may or may not have been entirely credible) that I learned that extroversion and introversion have absolutely nothing to do with how much a person talks. It has to do with energy.

Extroverts gain energy from being around people. They thrive on crowds. Introverts are the exact opposite. Being around too many people drains them of energy, and they have to spend time alone in order to recharge. That's where the Introverts-are-Loners stereotype comes in.

I've finally learned that I am an introvert. So are Oliver and Joni. The rest of the guys? They're extroverts through and through. They love this atmosphere. They love the people. They're all totally high on the energy of everyone around them here at the American Music Awards. And they should be. This is their night.

Right now, they're being interviewed. Lots of fans are screaming at them from the sidelines. The woman conducting the interview even seems flustered by their presence. It's probably not helping that Josh and Sam are both acting particularly flirty, winking, running their hands through their hair, you know.

"You guys have come so far in your short career. Tell me, how does it feel to be here at the AMAs?" she asks.

"Incredible," Josh answers. "This is just the most incredible feeling. We're so proud and we're just really excited to perform and have a good time tonight."

"This is just the beginning of a really exciting week for you. Your third album, *Meet Me on the Midway*, is due out in just a few short days. What can you tell us about it?"

"We can tell you that it's amazing," Cory grins.

The woman interviewing them laughs. "I'm glad to hear that. I hope you think it's amazing."

"Well like you said, this is our third album. The first two have been so well-received with the fans and we're so grateful to all of them for their love and support, and we just really hope that they love this album as much as they love the first two," Sam says.

"These songs are our love letter to them," Oliver adds.

"Speaking of love letters, your love lives have been crazy lately. Care to share any dirty details?"

"Don't believe everything you read online," Sam advises.

"Especially about me," Josh pipes up.

"Or me," Oliver adds.

"Everything they say about me is true," Jesse jokes.

"Same," Cory admits.

The interviewer laughs. "Well, boys, I hope you enjoy your evening. You truly deserve it."

"Thank you."

"Thanks a lot."

And with that, the guys are back to the lights, stars, and celebrity of the red carpet.

❀♫❀

Every time I watch the Oscars or the Emmys or any sort of awards ceremony, I always think about how strange it is to see so many actors together and out of context. Seeing Han Solo casually chatting with Sherlock Holmes and Catwoman can really throw you for a loop. I'm feeling the same way now, seeing so many different singers and musicians all together. Most of the time, they all seem to exist in their own separate universes.

Not here. Here, they're all packed together under one roof, and it's a little overwhelming. There's so much *talent* in this one room. It's strange to think about. How is this building still standing with all the star power inside?

Joni doesn't seem at all fazed by the famous faces all around her. Then again, Joni is kind of hard to impress. Me? I'm trying to remind myself to stay calm and pretend I'm cool. It's difficult. Seriously, how can I be expected to act cool and casual when the greatest names in music are in this room, some of them within mere feet of me? I know that by now, I should be kind of used to it, and with the guys, I totally am. But if you don't geek out even a little bit when Paul McCartney says hello to you, you might not be human.

By now, the show is about half over and the guys are the next group to perform. I don't know why, but I always get anxious whenever I watch them from the audience. Watching from backstage, I'm totally fine, but sitting out here? I'm a nervous wreck.

Of course, there's no reason for me to feel this way. The guys love performing live, and they're always amazing. Even when they mess up or fall down or accidentally botch the lyrics (often on purpose), they smile, laugh it off, and it goes down in fandom history, or at least on Buzzfeed, as yet another adorable and epic The Kind of September moment. Basically, the guys can do no wrong.

Okay, that's not entirely accurate. There are plenty of false rumors and bad information floating around about their personal lives. But as far as their career goes, they're gold. That becomes even clearer when they take the stage to the most enthusiastic ovation of the night.

Sam:
She's in love with autumn leaves
And the song the zephyrs sing
I don't know but I believe
That love will find her

Cory:
She tells me that she likes to play
When the skies are cold and gray
But I hope she'll find a way
To open up her heart
Please, baby, open up your heart

All:
And meet me, meet me
Where the lights are always shining
Meet me, meet me
On the Midway
Tell me, tell me
That our love will be forever

And we will be together, come what may
On the Midway

Josh:
I don't know what she thinks about
Her pretty head is filled with doubt
But I hope she'll figure out
How much I need her

Oliver:
She laughs away the dark of night
And her eyes are full of light
Oh, that she'd be mine tonight
I'd never let her go
No, I'll never let you go

All:
So meet me, meet me
Where the lights are always shining
Meet me, meet me
On the Midway
Tell me, tell me
That our love will be forever
And we will be together, come what may
On the Midway

Jesse:
You say you're scared of how you feel
And I can understand
But I know that this love is real
Just let me take your hand...

All:
So meet me, meet me
Where the lights are always shining
Meet me, meet me
On the Midway

Tell me, tell me
That our love will be forever
And we will be together, come what may
On the Midway.

Chapter Fourteen

"It's nights like these
In the summer
I remember
And I wonder
Are you here with me
Eleven summers
Passing slowly
Do you remember
To remember June..."

Song: "Remembering June"
Artist: The Kind of September
From the Album: *The Kind of September*

Note to self. It doesn't matter how cool the American Music Awards after-party is. If you have to wake up to catch an 8:00 AM flight, you're going to feel terrible. I know you thought you could handle it. You can't.

I'm not kidding you. I didn't know it was physically possible to be this exhausted. Honestly, I have no idea how the guys are even conscious right now. I only attended one after-party. They were invited to three! Granted, as Artist of the Year, they deserved to let loose and celebrate. But three after-parties?

I'm willing to bet they didn't even bother sleeping, but I haven't asked them. No one seems capable of actually making words.

This isn't fair. I didn't even drink.

The only person who is even kind of sort of awake and functional is Joni, but that's because she skipped all the after-parties and went straight back to our hotel after the awards were over. She's been trying to go over the schedule for after we land back in New York, but none of us are listening. I think I might have heard something about an interview and a photo shoot, but thankfully, no one wants to take pictures of me, so guess what?

I'm gonna sleep.

Honestly though, I know I sound like I'm complaining a lot, but I'm really, *really* happy for the guys and so proud of them. I know they're proud of all they've accomplished too, and they should be. Last night was awesome. This week is going to be spectacular. If the most I've got to complain about is that I only got a few hours of sleep last night, I'd say life is pretty okay.

"*Sam Morneau's Secret Affair,*" Joni announces out of the blue.

Wait, that doesn't sound okay.

"What?" Sam asks, looking like he just snapped out of a really weird dream and into an even weirder reality.

"*According to a number of witnesses, notorious heartbreaker, Sam Morneau, was seen flirting and partying with fellow pop sensation Chloe Conley,*" Joni reads from her phone. "*Friends of Conley, who famously dated Morneau's friend and bandmate, Josh Cahill, confirm that the two got cozy last night at one of the American Music Awards after-parties.*

"*'They seemed really into each other. It didn't seem to bother him at all that she's his friend's ex,' claims one source, who requested to remain anonymous.*

"*No word yet on how Cahill, who is often viewed as the most sensitive of the group –*"

"What?!" Josh exclaims.

"*– is handling this devastating betrayal.*"

126

"Are you kidding me?" Sam groans and leans his head back against the airport benches.

"Did you see Chloe Conley last night?" Joni asks him.

"For like, two seconds. We ran into each other, I told her I enjoyed her performance, she gave me a hug and that was it."

"See, where you went wrong was telling her you enjoyed her performance," Jesse remarks.

"Do people really think I'm the sensitive one?" Josh demands. His brows are furrowed and he looks like he's trying not to panic. I'm kind of beginning to think that he and I are a lot alike. We're both dwellers. "I'm not the sensitive one, am I?"

"Right now? Yes," Joni answers.

"I knew it. It's the big brown eyes, isn't it?"

"And the whiny personality. Shut up," Joni snaps. "How many times do I have to tell you guys to be careful? You know what kind of person Chloe Conley is. You guys just won Artist of the Year, and you're less than twenty-four hours away from your third album release. This is not at all the time for any sort of bad publicity."

"Well, it's a little late for that, apparently," Jesse comments. He sounds almost amused.

"Jesse?" Cory says.

"Yeah, bro?"

"Not helping."

"Look, I know you think I'm overreacting, and I know that this is just a big joke to you, but don't you understand what the problem is?" Joni asks.

The guys respond with blank stares. I'm not really even sure I understand what the problem is. Yes, I hate that Sam is the target of yet another fake scandal and I hate that these people persistently spread lies about him and the guys, but in all honesty, I really don't see any of that affecting their popularity or their record sales. They never have in the past.

"Is it because some crazy girl and her goons are spreading lies about us? Because that happens like, every day," Josh reminds her.

"But what's the difference here?" Joni asks. Again, the stares. I think Oliver and Sam are actually on the verge of dozing off. Joni heaves an exasperated sigh. Surely she's figured out by now that the guys have talent oozing out their ears, but when it comes to logic and actually having to think, the glass is half-full, at best. "The difference is that this time, they're pitting you against each other."

"So?" Josh asks, shrugging his shoulders.

"How do I explain this?" Joni rubs her eyes with the heels of her hands. "Mel. Why do you like reading those stupid young adult novels?"

"Hey, they're not stupid." That's totally offensive. I love young adult fiction. Maybe it's not as quote-unquote sophisticated as what Joni likes to read, but you know what? Those books make me happy. So there.

"Just answer the question," Joni tells me.

"I don't know. They're fun."

"But they're not all fun, are they? They've all got a bit of drama. A love triangle. Feuding mythical creatures. Maybe a romance with a dead person."

"What's your point?" I ask.

"The point is that those books wouldn't sell half as well if there wasn't *conflict*. These gossip columnists and reporters are the same way. No one wants to read a news article about a band who gets along. There has always got to be some kind of back-stabbing or friction, and if there isn't any, they're going to find a way to create some."

"Okay, that might be the case, but there is no friction. There's no inner turmoil. Sam didn't betray anyone. They can write that stuff all day long, Jo. It doesn't make it true," Jesse says.

"It's not true this time," Joni says, folding her arms across her chest.

"What, are you saying you think Sam is that guy? That he, or any of us, would actually do something like this? Come on, Joni, I thought you knew us better than that."

"Stop," Sam raises his voice. "Look, if Joni's right and the media wants to stir up some kind of tension between us, then they're doing a pretty good job. Jesse, you know that Joni is just trying to look out for us. Give her a break."

"Thank you, Sam," Joni says.

"You're welcome," Sam tells her. "And look, I'm just as sick of these lies as you are. But if we let them get to us, then the tabloids and everyone behind them win. And yeah, it's upsetting to think that some people will actually believe I would do this to a friend - "

"Not as upsetting as it is that people think I'm *devastated* by this so-called betrayal," Josh once again interjects.

" - *however*, we have too much going on this week. Too much *good* stuff. And I think that's what we need to be focusing on. Not this."

I'm not sure I've mentioned this, but Sam can be very eloquent when he wants to be. I mean yeah, most of the time, he's kind of gross or kind of silly or sometimes even mildly inappropriate, but he's got his head and his heart in the right place. That's not something I can say for a lot of people. I'm not even sure it's something I can say for myself.

"You know it's still going to come up," Joni warns them. "In all these interviews. They're going to be asking about this and not the album."

"And we'll deal with it," Sam assures her. "We always do."

"And as always, we'll charm them with our ravishing good-looks and devil-may-care charisma," Jesse says.

"And make it very clear that I am *not* the sensitive one."

"Josh, let it go."

While the guys are at their photo shoot, I'm taking the time to do some last-minute studying for my finals. And by that, of course, I mean I'm browsing all the social media sites to see how the fans are responding to the Sam/Chloe/Josh non-triangle.

It's funny. I always thought that drama like this ended in high school. But clearly, that's not the case. In fact, I'm tempted to say it only gets worse. In high school, all you have to worry about are grades and whether or not a cute boy likes you. Out in the real world, there are stupid things like money and reputations and status that make people go out of their already ridiculous minds.

Don't believe the lie, kids. There is no magical line that people cross once they reach the age of eighteen that magically transforms them into mature adults. They're all still the same, crazy, dramatic people, but with the legal ability to vote. Yay, America.

As before with the #*Meliver* debacle, there are fans who are jumping to Sam's defense. However, there are others who are accusing him of being a player. Several are in denial. A few are begging the masses to mind their own business. Unfortunately, those precious few are often lost beneath the hundreds of thousands of fans bemoaning their existence.

This time, however, I'm also noticing a bit of a new trend: the *We Hate Chloe Conley* trend.

I can't believe that @MsChloeConley would do this to Sam. I used to like her music. Now she makes me sick.

Chloe Conley's new album is coming out next month! No one buy it!

@MsChloeConley is literally the worst person I've ever heard of. #SupportSamMorneau

Even though I know Sam appreciates his fans sticking up for him, I also know that he would be the first person to tell them not to blame Chloe. I've never met her, so I have no idea what she's really like, but from what I've heard, it's the people working for her who fuel these continuous flames of fraudulence. Granted, that kind of means it's still on her for not firing them, but she doesn't seem to be a bad person. Even if she was, Sam still wouldn't want to see his fans criticizing a fellow musician. None of the guys would.

But while the fans aren't really saying anything new, the media is taking the reports to the next level.

Sam and Chloe's Backstage Passion!

The Ultimate Betrayal: Sam Morneau Hooking Up With Bandmate's Ex!

Is This the End of TKOS? Sam Morneau and Josh Cahill Feuding over Pop Princess Chloe Conley!

And wouldn't you know it? They're all the top news stories.

Joni was right. Angst sells. Too bad for the press, none of it's true. Well actually, it might be a good thing for them. If The Kind of September did happen to break up, then all their dramatic source material goes out the window. They'd have to rely on other celebrities to stir up trouble, and let's face, it, no one else does anything as scandalous as TKOS. Supposedly.

You know, it's kind of weird to think that for once, Tara isn't behind all this. Unless she got jealous that she wasn't invited to the awards themselves, let alone the after-parties, and went to all the news outlets as some sort of ill-conceived attempt at vengeance. But to tell you the truth, I don't think she's that smart.

Unfortunately, Cory still hasn't figured out that she isn't that smart because he's still dating her. Or maybe brains just aren't that important to him. Either way, Sam just texted me to let me know that Cory's invited her back to our hotel for the evening since, and I quote, she hasn't seen him in three whole days. Why can't he just go back to her hotel? Because the album is being released tonight at midnight and he wants her to be a part of the celebration.

Honestly, I don't know how much celebrating will be going on, since I got more sleep than all of them last night and

I can barely stand up straight. But they're guys. Even when we were kids, they seemed to have more energy than us girls. I don't know why. Maybe the estrogen slows us down or something.

I just got another text from Sam.

Are you still studying?

Yep, I reply. And of course, by that, I mean no. But I am still sitting in my room, in my sweats, on my computer, so I guess that sort of counts as studying.

Great. Be there in ten minutes.

As usual, I feel a tiny skip in my otherwise perfectly stable heartbeat. Being with Sam anytime is always wonderful, but being alone with him is the best.

Okay. See you soon. :)

Want food? he asks.

Oh, always.

Okay. I'll see what I've got in my stash.

Sam is kind of like a squirrel. Every once in a while, he goes on grocery raids where he stocks up on snack foods. He doesn't even look at what he buys. If he can eat it, it goes in the stash. The weird part is that none of us know where he keeps this secret food. It is a total mystery. As far as I know, he's never told a soul. May I just say that keeping a secret like that in a group like this is unprecedented. Privacy just doesn't exist in this environment, and yet none of us can find Sam's Secret Snack Stash. It's the one thing in the world that I don't know about him.

And you know what? I think he's pretty proud of it.

Chapter Fifteen

"They said you're a hero child
You're made of steel
You're flesh and blood
Of the lucky ones
Who make these legends real
It was in that shining moment
That I knew I had it all
That I had so far to fall..."

Song: "Legends"
Artist: The Kind of September
From the Album: *Meet Me on the Midway*

Sam arrives with enough junk food to feed a small army, or at least an entire class of poor college students. He's also changed out of his photo shoot clothes and into plaid pajama pants and an oversized t-shirt. This is how I like him best. Yeah, he's super sexy when he's in his suits and button-down shirts (especially when he's performing), but this is the Sam that I know. The one who likes to hang out and eat snacks in his pajamas and doesn't have to worry about what anyone says or thinks.

"Sorry I'm late. Had to wait until Cory was out of the room before I could grab the snacks," he says.

"Seriously, where do you keep all this?"

"I don't know," he offers an innocent grin.

"Come on, I'm not going to sneak into your room and steal it."

"I don't know that. Remember that time you stole a french fry off my plate?" He raises his eyebrows, like a parent scolding a misbehaving child.

"We were in eighth grade. You need to let that go."

"And you need to accept the fact that you just might be the reason I don't trust anybody with my food." Of course. His little food-hoarding act is my fault.

"Over one french fry?"

"You know how I feel about my fries."

It's true. Sam loves all food, but he's always been particularly fond of french fries. I should have known better than to take one. But best friends are supposed to share things with each other that we can't share with anybody else. That should include bad cafeteria food.

"You know, one day, someone is going to figure it out," I tell him.

"And when that day comes, I will find a new hiding place," Sam replies, flopping down onto my bed. I try not to think about how much I wish I was lying next to him. Don't guys realize what they do to us? I know they think that we're the ones who are impossible to understand, but come on. How can a sexy guy stretch out on a bed like that and *not* expect his female companion to feel a little flustered?

I guess it all goes back to the We've-Been-Friends-So-Long-He-Probably-Doesn't-Even-Realize-I'm-A-Girl theory. I'm sure most women are at least vaguely aware of this phenomenon. A guy and a girl grow up together and for some reason, one becomes completely genderless to the other. Like a giant colorless blob. That is me. I am the blob.

"So, how was the photo shoot?" I ask.

"There were lots of cameras," he replies. His eyes are closed and I'd almost think he was about to fall asleep except for the fact that he's munching away on a bag of Cheetos. Sam might be the most talented guy I know: he can sing, he can dance, and he can actually snack and nap at the same time.

"Are you getting Cheeto crumbs on my pillow?"

"Probably." Completely unapologetic. Seriously, why do I like him so much? Am I just that superficial that I can be swayed by a pair of gorgeous blue eyes and a playful grin?

Probably.

"I'm going to take a picture of you and put it on Twitter with the caption, 'Hey ladies, this is what actually happens when you get Sam Morneau into bed.'"

"They'll still think I'm adorable," he counters. Unfortunately, that's true.

Have you ever noticed that cute guys have it so much easier than the rest of us do? They can be gross, they can stink, they can do the stupidest, most embarrassing things and yet people still think they're precious. I've never met another person who could get away with half the things Sam does just because he's cute and charismatic.

Of course, they've also got the media trying to sabotage and vilify them at every twist and turn, so maybe charm does have its downsides.

By now, I'm sick of pretending to study. I've been sitting at this hotel desk all day, my back and neck are cramped up, my eyes are blurred from staring at a computer screen, and even though he's leaving me with a blanket full of Cheeto crumbs, I just want to spend time with Sam. I shut down my laptop and settle down on the bed next to him. He opens one eye and glances over at me.

"I thought you were studying."

"I need a break. Want to watch a movie?"

"Mmm..." he considers it. "Not really."

"Play 'Would You Rather?'"

"No."

"Okay. What do you want to do?"

"We could just talk," he says.

That's actually the best answer he could have given me.

"What do you want to talk about?"

"What are you most looking forward to about next year?" he asks. When I don't respond immediately, he explains, "That was one of our interview questions after the photo shoot."

"What did you say?"

"I said the tour. But I'm really looking forward to visiting places we haven't been yet." he says.

"Me too. I want to go to Alaska."

"Why Alaska?" he asks.

"Well, it's one of the few states we haven't been. It's beautiful. There's a lot of history and different cultures. It seems like the kind of place you'd go to have an adventure. And I'd finally get to see the Aurora Borealis."

"I remember you saying that when we were younger. That the first item on your bucket list was seeing the Northern Lights," he smiles. "You know you inspired the lyrics in 'Snowlight,' right?"

"What?" And just like that, I've forgotten how to breathe. I've never inspired anything before, let alone the lyrics to one of the most popular songs in the world. "I did?"

"Yeah. Your birthday is in the winter. And you've got that thing with the Northern Lights. I don't know. Snow has just always made me think of you."

"Really?"

"Yeah. I'll never forget the first time you saw it. Or at least, the first time I saw you see it. It was like nothing else in the world existed to you. You were just so enraptured with these little pieces of frozen water falling from the sky. It was kind of like seeing something magical."

"Sam..." I could probably live another eighty years and never again hear anything to make my heart melt like the words he just said to me. "Wow..."

"Did I just embarrass you?" he asks with another sleepy grin.

"No. I'm... I'm kind of speechless. 'Snowlight' is one of my favorite songs."

He shrugs. "It's for you."

And with that, I truly do not believe I will ever be happier than I am that this moment.

Of course, Sam's phone chimes about half a second later, snapping me out of my giddy stupor and back to a world in which other people, besides the two of us, exist.

He reaches into his pocket and lifts his phone up so that he's holding it directly above the bridge of his nose. You'd think he'd have learned from the dozen and a half times he's dropped it on his face while doing that, but apparently not.

"Do the guys need you?" I ask him.

"No. It's from Chloe."

"Conley?" I ask. Suddenly all residual feelings of euphoria from Sam's earlier revelation have vanished, leaving a cold sense of petty anger and a touch of jealousy in their place. "What does she want?"

"She's apologizing for all the reports and rumors."

"Really?" That's a new twist. As far as I know, she never texted Josh to apologize for all the trouble she caused him. Of course, that raises a brand-new question. "How did she get your number?"

"Who knows," Sam replies, typing out a response. I'm dying to ask what he's saying to her. Hopefully, it's something along the lines of *You should be sorry, leave me alone,* but Sam is way too nice for that. He's probably just telling her it was no big deal and that he appreciates her apology.

But you know, he could add in the *leave me alone* bit just to be safe.

After he finishes typing, he tosses his phone aside and closes his eyes again. I know I shouldn't be worried about what just happened. After all, it's not like he really knows Chloe at all. But she's still beautiful. And talented. And famous. And apparently, she's not as terrible a person as we all thought she was. I mean yeah, maybe she's lying and she's not really sorry. But what if she is a genuinely nice person?

And what if she and Sam keep texting? What if she turns out to be exactly his type and they fall in love and get married and have beautiful, talented, famous babies?

My head hurts.

Sam, on the other hand, is totally oblivious to my inner turmoil because he asks, "Do you think people will like the new album?"

"Yeah," I tell him honestly. "I think everyone is going to love it."

"Do you like it?"

"You know I do. I think it's your best so far."

"Really?"

"Really."

"You're not just saying that because you're my best friend?"

"Not just saying it," I promise him. "Why? Are you worried?"

"No. I just want the fans to like it."

"They will," I assure him.

I guess even though they receive words of affirmation and adoration from practically everyone they meet, it's still nice to hear it from people you know care about you. Strangers constantly profess their love for Sam, and he offers declarations of love in return, but I think every once in a while, all the guys need to be reminded that they have friends and family members who knew and loved them before all this, and who would still love and appreciate them even if they weren't The Kind of September.

Sure enough, he whispers, "Thank you, Mel," before he drifts off to a well-deserved and much-needed sleep.

❀♪♩❀

It's almost nine o'clock in the evening. I didn't realize how much time has passed until Joni texted me a few minutes ago asking if Sam and I were coming to the party.

Okay, technically, this midnight release celebration isn't a real party. It's just our usual group, hanging out, listening to the new album, drinking champagne, and live-tweeting. There will also be a lot of food. Good thing too, since my growling stomach just reminded me that I haven't eaten dinner yet.

The point is, even though the release shindig isn't an actual party, it's still going to be a lot of fun.

Yeah, we're coming, I type back to her before glancing over at Sam, who is still passed out on my bed. He did quite a bit of muttering after he first fell asleep, but after a while, he just started snoring. Not obnoxiously, but just loud enough to distract me from my millionth attempt at studying. Thankfully, I have a brand-new pair of headphones that come in quite handy when I need to tune something, or someone, out.

Please hurry. Cory just told me that Tara is on her way. Ugh.

Oh boy. I can't wait to see her again.

Setting my phone down on the desk, I walk over to Sam and gently shake his shoulder.

"Sam," I whisper. I don't know why, but I always feel so bad about waking people up. It feels so disruptive. But there's no way I'm going to face Tara without him. That, and I know he really wants to be there for the release.

"Hmm?" he murmurs and opens up a sleepy eye.

"Joni just texted me. The party's about to start."

"What time is it?" he asks, rubbing his eyes and sitting up. His voice is low and rough, just as it always is right after he wakes up.

"Almost nine."

"Oh wow... I was out," he remarks.

"You needed it," I tell him. "But you should know that you talk in your sleep and now I know all your secrets."

"Oh yeah?" he grins.

"Yep. You told me everything. Right down to where you keep your secret food."

"That's not very nice. You're not supposed to exploit a man when he's sleeping," he teases me.

"What better time to exploit?" I ask.

"Touché."

Once he's fully awake and I've made at least a tiny attempt to look like I didn't spend an entire day sitting in front of a computer, we walk together down the hall and to Jesse, Josh, and Oliver's room. The new album is already playing through Jesse's enormous pair of speakers that he brings with him everywhere, a makeshift buffet is spread out on a collapsible table and Josh is running around hugging everybody.

"Mel, Sam, there you are!" he greets us and plants a huge kiss on my cheek.

Thirteen, I count silently.

"Are you guys stoked or what? Third album, baby!" Josh asks.

If Josh acts this much like a frat guy when he's sober, I can't wait to see what kind of effect alcohol will have on him. Then again, he might not drink. He has that weird thing with soft drinks. He might not like the burn of alcohol either. Of course, Josh really doesn't need to drink. He's constantly drunk on life.

"Yeah!" Sam exclaims. Josh's enthusiasm is contagious, but I have something else on my mind.

"Can I have some food?" I ask.

"Jeez Mel, way to make our night of self-congratulatory festivities all about you," Josh huffs. "What are we going to do with her, Sam?"

"Unfortunately, I think she's beyond help at this point, Josiah."

"That's so sad. She had so much potential."

"You guys are so sweet," I tell them. Honestly, though, I love that we can all give each other a hard time. In a weird way, I think it's a sign of genuine friendship and affection. If I can give you a hard time, that must mean I really like you and feel comfortable around you. The guys are the same way.

I make my way over to Joni, who is standing with Cory and Oliver next to the buffet table. Okay, I was really going for the food, but I'm glad that Joni is there, too. The two of us need to stick together when Tara finally graces us with her ever-delightful presence.

"Having fun?" I ask, piling a few miniature sandwiches and a handful of baby carrots and ranch dip onto a plate.

"For now," she remarks and folds her arms across her chest. See, this is why I'm glad I have Joni. I'm typically not a very surly person, but there's still a lot of stuff that bothers me. But I know I can always depend on her to adequately express exactly whatever negative emotion I might be feeling so that I don't have to.

When you think about it, it works.

"You said you would be happy this evening," Cory reminds her in the annoying sing-song voice that he reserves specifically for her.

"I said I'd try," she sings back to him as Jesse suddenly appears beside her.

"Wave, everyone! You're on Facetime with my mom!" he announces, holding up his phone. Mrs. Scott smiles back at us from his screen.

We greet her with a chorus of, "Hi!" "Hello, there!" "Hi, Mama Scott!"

"Hi, kids!" she replies. "I just wanted to let you know how proud I am of all of you and how much I love you!"

"Aw, we love you, too!" Cory responds.

It's one of The Kind of September's better kept secrets that tall, sexy, rock star Jesse Scott is the group's biggest Mama's Boy. I'm not kidding. Seeing him with his mom is one of the cutest things you will ever witness. He is so protective of her and he is her world, her pride and joy, and she almost loves us just as much.

I sometimes think it's weird that so many people know so many intimate details about the guys and their families. But then, I also think it's kind of a tragedy that they don't know more.

Before I can dwell any further, Cory's phone chimes. The grin on his face confirms what the rest of us already know.

Tara's here.

Chapter Sixteen

"In this world of mirrors
And crystal clear delusions
Love is all in what you see
But you hide behind a smokescreen
These colors drowning out
And these shapes all seem to fade
And I'm struggling to see
Beyond your smile, beyond your smokescreen..."

Song: "Smokescreen"
Artist: The Kind of September
From the Album: *17 Times Over*

I'll be the first to admit that I don't like confrontation, so waiting for Cory to return with his girlfriend who kind of hates my guts has got me a little agitated. I'm trying not to let it show because as Josh so deliberately pointed out, tonight is supposed to be about celebrating the new album. I don't want to ruin it for the guys who have worked so hard for this moment, but also countless hours of their time. They deserve to enjoy tonight.

Sam and Joni both know that I'm nervous. Even though neither has said so, I can tell by the way they're hovering around me, like they're protecting me. Then again, I'm still standing next to the buffet table. Maybe they're just hungry. Sam is in the process of scarfing down what must be his eighth chocolate chip cookie.

Whatever the reason, I'm glad I have them close to me. It's kind of like having bodyguards. Albeit, rather useless ones, but bodyguards nevertheless.

When Cory finally returns with Tara, I'm unpleasantly surprised to see that she's brought along a plus-one: her wannabe singing sensation BFF, Courtney Vickers.

"Hey, guys!" Tara greets us. She looks so happy to be there that for a moment, I'm hopeful that maybe, just maybe, she's forgotten that I exist. I'm even more encouraged when she says, "You all remember Courtney, don't you?"

"I sure do," Jesse winks.

Courtney giggles, but the minute her eyes lock on Sam, it's like the rest of us don't exist.

"Sam!" she exclaims, model-walking over to us. I'm not kidding. The way she glides across the room reminds me of a model on the catwalk; her steps pointed and deliberate, her thick auburn hair dancing behind her. "It's good to see you again."

"Yeah, you too," he replies through a mouthful of cookie.

"I love the new album. I think it's your best yet."

"Thanks. We like it too."

"You're so great," Courtney giggles and taps him on the shoulder. He glances down at his arm, almost like he's checking to make sure her touch didn't leave a mark. Courtney doesn't seem to notice. "Hey, um... I'm sorry, what's your name again?" she asks me.

"Mel," I reply.

"Oh right! You're the one who's dating Oliver!"

"Yeah, except we're not dating."

"You're not?"

"No."

"You mean you hang out with him all the time, you obviously like each other, and you haven't hooked up with him yet?" She sounds perplexed and for some reason, disappointed.

Sam, meanwhile, sends a curiously amused smirk my way.

"We don't like each other. Not like that. We're just friends," I tell Courtney.

"Well, it definitely didn't look that way in the pictures that Tara showed me. What, are you leading him on?"

Me leading Oliver on. The thought is so ludicrous on so many levels.

"No. We were talking. Sometimes friends talk."

"Well, I think you'd be really cute together," Courtney insists.

"Oliver's British. He'd be cute with anyone," Sam comments. The man makes a valid argument.

"Well, whatever. Listen Mel, would you take a picture of me and Sam?" Courtney asks. "You don't mind, do you, Sam?"

"No, not at all."

I oblige, even though I'm know Courtney will probably use the image for her own interests of fame and self-promotion. Oh well. Maybe it will help deter the Chloe Conley rumors.

In other parts of the room, Joni is sticking close to Josh and Oliver while Jesse third-wheels it again with Tara and Cory. Tara, strangely enough, keeps looking over at Courtney and fidgeting, almost like she's annoyed. Watching Tara's odd body language, I begin to wonder if maybe she didn't bring Courtney for Sam this time, but for Jesse. If that's the case, then either Courtney didn't get the memo or she simply doesn't care, because she still only has eyes for Sam. In all fairness, I do too, but come on. A set-up with Jesse Scott is a pretty sweet deal. I'd have a huge crush on Jesse if he wasn't Sam's friend and Joni's ex.

I've never admitted it to anyone, but I did have a dream once that Jesse and I were making out in the back of the tour bus. It was totally innocent (sort of), but I still couldn't look him or Joni in the eye for about a week.

"Why is she here?" The loud and rather aggressive voice snaps me out of my admittedly pleasant memories of that dream and back to the hotel room, where I find myself the center of unwanted attention.

"Baby, calm down. You know she's a friend." Cory tries to soothe the savage beast, but to no avail. I seem to recall him telling me something along the lines of Tara really is sorry about everything that happened. Either she's forgotten that she's sorry or Cory is completely full of it.

Don't ask me why, but I'm thinking it's the latter.

"Why would you still her want her hanging around after what she said about me?" Tara demands.

"Wait, is she the one who - "

"Yes!" Tara answers before Courtney can even finish asking the question. Am I the one who what?

"Oh my God. I thought you were nice." Courtney is suddenly looking at me like she's just unmasked me, like one of the villains on *Scooby Doo.*

"Hey, she is nice. She's a good person," Sam argues, stepping up to my defense.

"Didn't you hear about what she said to Tara?" Courtney asks.

"Yeah, but I also know that your friend was running around and spreading lies about her personal life."

Wow. In all the years we've been friends, I've never heard Sam talk like that to anyone. It's so brave. So chivalrous.

So romantic.

"I didn't appreciate that either, for the record," Oliver speaks up.

"So that's it. She mouths off to me like a whiny, snot-nosed brat and you're just going to act like it never happened?"

"No, no, we sat her down and had a long discussion about it," Jesse assures her.

"Yeah. Sam gave her a spanking and everything," Josh remarks with a suggestive and mischievous grin.

At this moment, I'm thankful I don't have any food or drink in my mouth, because I would undoubtedly be choking on it. I can *not* believe Josh just said that. In front of the entire group. In front of Tara. In front of *Sam*. Who, incidentally, doesn't look even the least bit fazed by Josh's inappropriate insinuation.

Tara and Courtney, however, are suddenly zeroing in on Sam and me. I wait for them to throw out a new accusation, but before either can speak, Sam says, "Mel and I are not together."

I can't tell you why, but his words cut through me like a knife. Even though it's the truth and that he has no reason to say otherwise, hearing him actually speak those words, for some reason, shatters even the fantasy I have of him possibly loving me back one day. Maybe it's not the words themselves, but the way he says it, with absolute assurance. No one could misinterpret them if they tried.

"But you like her, don't you?" Tara says, narrowing her eyes.

"Not like that. She's my friend. That's all we've ever been and all we're going to be."

Another blade to the heart. I hope I don't look as devastated as I feel, because if I do, then every person in this room is going to know that I'm in love with Sam Morneau. Even worse, they're going to pity me because now we all know for certain that he doesn't love me back. I want to get out of here, but I know that if I bolt, that will reveal the truth about me even faster than the pitiful look on my face.

"Besides," Sam continues. "There's someone else."

And with that, my heart officially breaks.

❀♪❀

Sam won't tell us who she is, but I have a feeling I already know. Of all the girls he's been linked to in the past few weeks, there's only one with whom he's had any sort of real human contact. Incidentally, she also happens to be the one the rest of his band mates can't stand. Chloe Conley. If Sam were to ever admit out loud that he had feelings for her, Josh, Jesse, Oliver, and even Cory would surely give him all sorts of hell.

I knew this would happen eventually, but why did it have to happen tonight?

Granted, this isn't the first time Sam has expressed interest in another girl. After all, he's had two girlfriends before, and one was even kind of a celebrity, but not a celebrity like Chloe Conley. She's on the A-List. She's talented, she's famous, and everyone (with the exception of Cory, apparently) loves her music. She also happens to be unbelievably beautiful. Her long, perfect hair is lighter than mine, like the color of milk chocolate mixed with honey and her eyes are an amazing shade of hazel-gray. I didn't even know that color existed. She's tall and slender and the worst part is I'm pretty sure she's all natural. She's flawless all on her own. She's exactly the kind of girl Sam *should* be dating. They're in the same league.

I mean, really. How have I deluded myself this long into thinking I actually had a chance with him? Yeah, he's my best friend and yes, we have a lot of history, and in a lot of ways, he's still the same guy he always was. But he's also different. I guess we all are in some respects, but he and the guys... their whole worlds changed the minute their first album hit the charts. It only makes sense that they would evolve too.

Sometimes I wonder what would have happened to us if The Kind of September hadn't happened. Would Sam and I be together? Would we have gone to the same college? Would we even still be friends? I think we would. I like to think that our friendship matters enough to endure. But who knows? All I know is that in spite of all the downfalls, I still think The Kind of September was supposed to happen. I think this experience has made all of us happier, and hopefully a lot of fans happier, than any of us could have ever imagined. And no matter what happens, I think I'm always going to be thankful for what all this experience has brought us.

Even if that experience also comes with watching Sam fall in love with another girl. I can't wish that none of this had ever happened, not for my sake, and certainly not for their sake. They have too many wonderful things going for them. I hope that I do too. Even if that means I'm never going to have Sam all to myself.

Though I guess in this world of renown and beauty and shining stars, I never was anyway.

"Are you okay?" Oliver asks me once we get a minute alone. Cory, Jesse, Tara, and Courtney are all out on the balcony, taking pictures of the scenery and Sam, Josh, and Joni are huddled in a corner on their respective phones and tablets. They each probably have about three social media sites going at once.

"Did you know?" I ask him.

"No. He's never said a word. But that's like him, you know? He doesn't like to talk about his personal life."

"I know." It is like him. It's totally like him. Even when he was dating his previous girlfriends, he wasn't keen on sharing any of the details. For which, I've got to be honest, I'm thankful. No girl wants to listen to the guy they love talk about his romantic exploits with a person who isn't her.

"Do you think it's Chloe?" Oliver asks me.

"I can't imagine who else it would be," I reply.

"Well, maybe she doesn't feel the same way."

It's nice that he's trying, but honestly, is there a girl alive who *wouldn't* date Sam Morneau? I kind of doubt it. Besides, her people already tried to hook her up with one member of the group. Clearly it's something she wants or she would have told them not to do it again.

"Thanks, Oliver," I say. And I mean it. It's nice having someone who knows how I feel and who, I'm pretty sure, is rooting for me. At least, I'd like to think so. I'm definitely rooting for him and Joni.

As the hours pass, Sam doesn't mention his mystery girl, but I can tell that he's feeling awkward having confessed. I try my best to act like there's absolutely nothing bothering me or wrenching my heart or crushing my soul, but I don't know if I'm doing a very good job. Thankfully, everyone is more focused on the countdown to midnight and the release to notice.

When midnight finally does arrive, there's a lot of cheering, hugging, and clinking of crystal glasses full of champagne. The guys take a group picture and tweet it out to all their fans. I want to enjoy myself, but by this point, I'm completely drained, both physically and emotionally. All I want to do is go back to my own room and crawl into bed like the sad, pathetic blob that I am.

Of course, when I do get into bed, I'll have to wipe away all the Cheeto crumbs that Sam so graciously left on my pillow. Seriously, how rude was that? He had the nerve to leave a mess on my bed even though he *doesn't* have feelings for me? That might seem like odd logic, but when it comes to guys, nothing makes sense. The male brain, I'm convinced, is the greatest mystery of life, the true final frontier.

Before I leave, I give each of the guys a hug, saving Sam for last out of habit. He holds me longer than the rest of his bandmates, long enough for me to breathe in his familiar scent. For some reason, the smell brings tears to my eyes. I almost feel like I'm saying goodbye to him, which is ridiculous because I'll see him again in just a few hours. It's like saying goodbye to a dream that was never mine in the first place.

Love is the worst.

Chapter Seventeen

"Heaven's eyes are wide tonight
And I can see you
I can see you
This starship's sailing across the sky
And I can see you
I can see you
Oh won't you come with me
Across a never-ending sea..."

Song: "Starship Sailing"
Artist: The Kind of September
From the Album: *17 Times Over*

Today is going to be a long day. Not only because it's the day of the big *Meet Me on the Midway* release celebration on *Good Morning America* and the guys have events scheduled literally from dawn until dusk, but because despite being totally exhausted last night, I barely slept. That's because my stupid mind wouldn't shut up about Sam and Chloe. I wonder if she's texted him any more. I wonder if he's called her. I wonder if they've made plans to see each other over the holidays. We'll be back in California in just a few days. She's probably waiting for him.

Of all the gossip and all the rumors and all the speculations, why did this have to be the time they were actually right?

Furthermore, someone (and by someone I mean Tara and Courtney) let it slip on a number of social media sites that Sam confirmed his relationship with Chloe. So now, instead of focusing on the new album and favorite songs and their upcoming tour, fans and reporters all across the globe are obsessing over Sam and Chloe, or as the fans are calling them, Mornley. Sam and Chloe's first names don't go all that well together, you see, so fans have resorted to combining their last names, Morneau and Conley. Thus, Mornley.

I have to admit though, some of the Twitter posts are pretty creative.

It's official. Sam is dating Chloe Conley. My heart hurts. #Mourning4Mornley

Seriously? Sam could have anyone. ANYONE. Why Chloe the CON-ley?

Mornley sounds like something you'd name a troll. #SamAndChloe #CanThisNotBeAThing

I wonder if Sam knew what he was getting himself into last night. I want to check on him, to make sure he's okay, but I know he and the rest of the guys are already in the dressing room, getting primped for the show. They'll be performing three songs off the new album this morning, followed by a reception, and then they're off to a series of interviews.

And then, just when it seems like it will never end, that's it. Today is our last day in New York for a while. Good thing, too. It has been snowing non-stop for the last few days, and the constant clouds are doing nothing for my bitter mood. Thankfully tomorrow, we're back on a plane to sunny Los Angeles, where the guys will at least have one day off before diving back into interviews and appearances on a few more talk shows. Only after all that's over will they finally get a real break before the tour kicks off after the beginning of the year. And they need a break. Not just from working, from everything. From this whole world of fame and photographs and false rumors. And, as it turns out, true rumors. They need some time to just be themselves.

But for now, the stage awaits.

❀♫♪❀

I can't tell you where I was or what I was doing the moment I realized that the guys had made it, like really made it. I think at first, we were all too afraid to believe it. Like, maybe it was all just a fluke. Maybe what seemed to be a big deal at the time really wasn't that big a deal in the grand scheme of things and in just a few weeks, it would all be over. But their fanbase has only grown. It's extraordinary.

Now, seeing the way they've filled up Times Square to watch their favorite band perform on *Good Morning America* absolutely takes my breath away.

Watching the guys run out on stage to the wild screams and cheers of their adoring audience, I actually feel myself begin to tear up. I'm so, so proud of them and I'm so caught up in the moment that I almost forget I'm supposed to be working.

I have the telephoto lens today. I'm supposed to be taking up-close pictures of the guys, as well as intimate shots of the stage and scenery. I love my job. It's wonderful and I wouldn't trade it for the world, but I also love watching them perform. Sometimes, I wish I could just sit and enjoy the show like everyone else.

All the guys look and sound amazing, and they are clearly having the time of their lives. I try my hardest not to focus too much on Sam, knowing that if I do, I'll probably make some kind of a scene, but it's difficult. He looks so good in his dark jeans and tan button-down shirt. Curse him for looking so good and for being such an attractive person in general. Especially when he dances around the stage and runs his fingers through his hair and does all of that other sexy musician stuff.

It's really quite irritating.

However, his antics do provide a very welcome distraction from the frigid temperatures out here. It's freezing. Thankfully, there isn't any precipitation, but the skies are thick with gray clouds and the wind chill has got to be in the teens. I'm telling you I cannot feel my ears, my nose, or my fingers.

I may be fascinated by the idea of snow and the Aurora Borealis, but when it all comes down to it, my poor California body just isn't cut out for this whole winter business.

Still, the show is amazing, and the fans are nothing short of wildly enthusiastic. I think it shows real dedication on their part, to brave the inclement weather to come out and happily support their favorite band. I know the guys appreciate it. They're always so nervous that instances of extreme weather will discourage fans from coming out to see them, but that's never been the case. If there is anything that can be said about The Kind of September's fans, it's that they are loyal. Loyal and incredibly supportive. It's like having a huge extended family. They don't only brave the crazy weather, they are happy to do so. I think that really says a lot about the guys, to have fans who love them that much.

After the show, we're off to the reception. The guys only have about thirty minutes to eat and mingle before their afternoon of, yes, more interviews and appearances, but at least I get a little bit of time with them. I haven't actually seen them all day.

"Hey," I greet Sam with a huge hug, even though the little voice in the back of my mind keeps reminding me that it's only temporary. I'm just a placeholder for Chloe Conley. And I'm really trying not to think about it. Once he lets me go, I tell him, "You all were amazing."

"You think they liked it?"

"They loved it."

His smile lights up his entire face, which, in spite of have just performed in the cold New York air, is flushed and damp with sweat. His hair is windswept and messier than ever, but his big blue eyes are bright and lively, almost electric. This is a moment that he and the guys have been waiting for for a long time. He's earned that smile.

"Melissa!" Jesse comes up behind me and claps a hand on my shoulder. He's not much of a hugger. "So, how were we?"

"You were great. As always. But everyone thought you were ugly," I reply. Sam guffaws. He doesn't laugh. He actually guffaws. Jesse just glares at me.

"Why are you so mean to me, Melissa?"

"Because she's cute and she can get away with it." Sam grins.

If I'd heard that from anybody else under any other circumstances, I'd think they were flirting. But I'm pretty sure Sam is just on an after-performance high right now. He'd probably call Jabba the Hutt cute if he were to roll into the room with his creepy dead alien eyes and his nasty slug mouth.

Of course, all the guys are really big *Star Wars* fans so Sam might think he's cute anyway. You never know.

Flirting and scary space worms aside, the reception is pretty fantastic. Not to mention all of the food they've prepared, which, I've got to be honest, probably costs more than I make working for the number one band in the nation. Granted, I'm really only compensated for my services with free food, free boarding, and complimentary trips around the world. The point is the food is expensive.

No sooner have Sam, Jesse, and I filled up our plates with coconut prawns, avocado wraps, and gourmet quiche than Joni approaches us, looking haggard.

"Have any of you checked Twitter recently?" she asks.

"You know, I meant to, but I had this thing where I had to be up on stage and singing - "

"Shut up, Jesse," Joni snaps. "Ever since the news broke about Sam and Chloe, people have been flooding not only her, but her fans also, with all kinds of cyber abuse. She's even had death threats."

"Are you kidding me?" I ask.

"Oh God, this is all my fault," Sam mutters, rubbing his forehead.

"It's not your fault. It's Tara's fault. But unfortunately, it is your problem," Joni tells him. "Look, I know that fans can be passionate. It's not unusual for them to get jealous, even possessive. The Internet makes that easy. But we can't have this."

"No, I definitely agree," Sam says. "I'll post something, try to put a stop to it."

"Good. Thank you."

Once she's gone, Sam sighs and says, "This was not supposed to happen."

"Bro, like she said, it's not your fault," Jesse says. "It's what always happen. It's what's always gonna happen. Should it? No way. But you can't control what other people say or do, especially online. Don't let it discourage you. You deserve to be happy."

"I guess," Sam replies, before wandering off, staring intently at his phone.

"Do you think he's going to be okay?" I ask Jesse.

"Oh yeah. He'll be fine. The real question is are you going to be okay?"

"Me? Why me?"

"If all this Sam and Chloe stuff turns out to be real." And then, with a cheeky wink, he walks away.

❀♪❀

Why did he say that? Why would he say that? Of course, he had to mean that because Sam is my best friend and if he gets a famous girlfriend then it's going to be weird for me. That has to be what he meant. Any other alternative is unthinkable. Because if Jesse knows, that means there's a very good chance that Josh and Cory know too. And if Jesse, Josh, Cory, and Oliver all know, then it's almost absolutely certain that Sam knows. That could be either a good or a bad thing.

It's a good thing because it means that even though he knows that I'm in love with him, he's still willing to be my friend and not high-tailing it in the other direction or living in fear that I'll give him cooties or something. It's a bad thing because it means he definitely doesn't feel the same way, like even a little bit. I mean, I know that last night, he kind of confirmed that he didn't feel that way about me, but you know. A girl still tries to hope.

But by now, I think it's safe to say my hope is wearing pretty thin. If there's any of it left at all.

I need to stop obsessing over this. Sam is not my life. So what if he knows that I like him, and so what if he's actively ignoring this fact in order to keep things normal between us, and *so what* if he's in love with the beautiful, talented, and totally in his league Chloe Conley? I have a lot of stuff going for me. I still have a great job with the one of the best bands around. I've traveled all over the world and I'm going to get to see even more of it in the coming year. I might even pass my online classes. I say might because it's definitely up in the air, but it would be an accomplishment.

So you see? I don't need Sam. I don't need any man. I could be single for the rest of my life and be okay with it. So there.

Right now, the guys are giving what must be their sixth or seventh interview for the day. I'm only sort of listening. It's nothing I haven't heard before. Tell us about the album. Tell us about the tour. Yeah, yeah, we get it. They're cool. Whatever.

I'm more interested in what's going on with the fans and the media and The Great Chloe Revolution.

Okay, so maybe I still care a little about what goes on with Sam.

That message he wrote out to fans earlier is very vague.

@SamMorneauTKOS: Remember, not everything you read online is true. Please be respectful.

And that's it. I guess it's really not all that surprising. If there's one thing Sam hates, it's discussing his personal life on Twitter. Actually, he just hates discussing his personal life in general.

Joni isn't satiated. She doesn't think he's trying hard enough. But I think at least some of the fans got the message.

#TKOS Family, please stop harassing Chloe and her fans. Come on, we're better than this.

I think we hurt Sam. Come on, he likes Chloe. He would never treat any of us this way. #HaveSomeRespect

I can't believe the way people have been bullying Chloe. This isn't us. #SupportSamAndChloe

But there are still others out there who are ignoring him.

Chloe Conley is rich, famous, and dating Sam Morneau. I don't feel sorry for her at all. So a few people said mean things to her. #BooHoo #CryMeARiver

If you ask me, it sounds like Sam is regretting his decision to date Chloe. Probably a publicity stunt. Who's shocked?

And so on.

Unfortunately, as Sam has said time and time again, this is a thing. And it's a thing that happens more frequently than it should. It's horrible that he and the fans go through this every time he likes or is reported to like someone. It's not fair to anyone, especially the ones being bullied. But even Sam doesn't have the power to put a complete stop to it.

It's hard to believe, but there are things that even the guys can't do.

Chapter Eighteen

"Maybe this time, time, time
We can make this last forever
And baby we'll shine, shine, shine
Just like these city lights
Oh please, be mine, mine, mine
In the moonlight, off the boardwalk
Over highways, under city lights tonight..."

Song: "City Lights"
Artist: The Kind of September
From the Album: *Meet Me on the Midway*

I don't sit next to Sam on our flight back to LA. I'm not sure if he thinks too much into it or if he even notices at all. As a guy, he probably doesn't. Like I said, they don't usually analyze things the way we do. They're so lucky.

But because I'm a girl and I do overanalyze things, I thought that it might be a better idea, all things considered, to take a seat next to Joni and let Sam sit with the guys. After all, I wouldn't feel right holding his hand knowing that Chloe Conley might very well be waiting for him to land in Los Angeles, where he'll sweep her off her feet and into a whirlwind romance that most girls, myself included, only dream about.

But, as I keep reminding myself, I don't care about that. I don't care about anything at all. We have a few short days in Los Angeles and then we get to go home for a whole month. I don't even remember the last time we had that much time off. It's going to be glorious. I'll be able to spend time with my family, play on the beach with my brother and sister, go shopping with my mom, maybe do some hiking in the Redwoods.

Yep. It's going to be a good holiday.

Now if I can just get through these next couple of days. I think I'll be able to. No. I know I'll be able to. Because if Melissa Kearney Parker is anything, it's determined.

Okay, that might be a lie. Maybe determination isn't my defining character trait. It's probably something more like neutralism. Or neuroticism. Some "ism" beginning with N-E-U.

Whatever. It doesn't matter. And dwelling any further on it isn't going to make my head any less chaotic. It fact, it will probably only make this worse. So I decide to try to make some small talk with Joni.

"So, do you and Cory have anything planned for the holidays?"

"Just spending as much time with our family as possible. Cory wants Tara to come stay with us for a few days and get to know the family, but thankfully, Mom thinks about as much of her as you and I do. She's been busy coming up with a whole list of reasons why we won't have time for guests."

"He's really serious about her, isn't he?"

"He thinks he is, but that's because he's too stupid to know the difference between love and infatuation."

"Aren't we all?" I ask. I mean, look at me. I'm infatuated with Sam and have been practically my entire life. I've always thought it was love. But maybe it's not. Maybe I'm just as stupid as everyone else and won't actually know what love really is until I'm on my deathbed. Maybe not even then.

"It's not hard to figure out. Infatuation is temporary. It's being in love with the idea of a person rather than the person him or herself. That's what Cory feels for Tara. He's in love with who he thinks she is, but he's not in love with her. How could he be?"

It's a fair question, I have to admit. But I understand what she's saying. When Cory looks at Tara, he sees an angel. He sees a beautiful girl who cares about him and wants to be with him. He doesn't see what the rest of us see. Maybe he can't. Or maybe, just maybe, he's choosing not to.

So where does that leave me? Have I simply been in love with my idea of Sam and not Sam himself? Perhaps I'm naive, but I really don't think so. I know Sam. I know everything about him. I know his faults, his quirks, his annoying tendencies. I've been with him through the highs and lows, the brightest moments and darkest days. And after all of that, I still find myself looking forward to waking up each and every morning, just because I know I'll get to spend time with him. He can make my entire day with a single smile. I'd do anything for him, and deep down, I'm pretty sure he'd do anything for me. He might not feel the same, but there's no doubt in my mind that what I've felt for Sam Morneau all these years is love.

And unfortunately for me, I'm fairly certain it's never going to go away.

❀♪❀

When we land in Los Angeles, the guys prepare for an appearance on a late-night talk show while I lock myself in Joni's and my hotel room in order to take my online exams. Both are due tonight, and even though I really haven't been concentrating on them the way I should, I think I'll do okay.

Sitting here alone at the desk, notebooks spread before me, I find my thoughts drifting to my high school days with Joni, Cory, Jesse, and Sam. Most of the time, it feels like a whole other life, but on occasion, it seems like only yesterday. I can still see Sam in his jeans and old t-shirts, dashing through the halls because he's late for class. I can hear Jesse telling a joke at his locker, his hair short and well-groomed. I commiserate with Cory as he frets over our physics projects that are due at the end of the week. Joni, on the other hand, isn't worried at all. She's a great student.

I have to admit sometimes I miss those days. They were simpler. A lot simpler. But even though I do find myself nostalgic at times, I don't think I'd go back to them. This life may be hectic, crazy, even downright chaotic, but it's also exciting and enlightening and so very full. I wouldn't trade this life for anything, even if Sam isn't a part of it the way I'd like him to be.

He must know somehow that I'm thinking about him, because I just received a text message from him asking, as usual, what I want for dinner later.

Just a few more days, I remind myself. *A few more days of food on the road and then I get a whole month of home-cooked meals and nutritious snacks.*

I know when we're kids, we dream of eating pizza and candy and other junk food all the time, but as an adult, it gets old. It's a good thing we're all constantly on the move or else we'd all weigh a ton. And when I say a ton, I don't mean a lot, I mean like, an actual ton. Like two thousand pounds. Each.

I finally finish both my exams around the same time I receive two texts, one from Joni and one from Sam. Each is informing me that the interviews are finished and that they're bringing Thai food back to the hotel. I tell them to hurry up. All that thinking and schoolwork left me famished.

While I wait, I can't help but wonder what the guys talked about on the show. What questions were they asked? I know they talked about the new album, but did the person interviewing them ask Sam about Chloe? He probably did. I wonder what Sam told him. The show doesn't air until the next day, and I'm almost positive the guys won't want to watch it. They're weird about watching themselves on television. I guess I'll just have to keep an eye on Twitter later.

No. I don't need to check Twitter later. I don't care about Sam and Chloe. I keep forgetting that I'm trying to take this as an opportunity to move on from Sam, even though I pretty much concluded earlier on the plane that I am, in fact, actually in love with him. But you know, maybe that doesn't matter. I hear all the time that it's possible to love more than one person. That the whole idea of The One is just a myth. I guess a part of me believes it. The problem though, is that while there might be more than one The One, there is only one Sam. No one else in the world is like him. So maybe one day, I will love someone else. Maybe I will even be *in* love with someone else. But I will never love anyone the way I love Sam.

And I know that sounds all kinds of romantic and everything, but to be honest with you, it kind of sucks.

❀♫♪❀

I'm tired of being cooped up in the hotel room, so I decide to head down to the lobby to wait for everyone. Besides, I've been sitting all day and I need to stretch my legs. I might even stop by the vending machines to grab a chocolate bar. Or two. Or maybe even five. After a day full of exams and emotional upheaval, I think I deserve a Snickers.

I've just collected my candy when Josh, Jesse, and Cory meander in through the revolving door.

"Hey, there's the scholar!" Cory greets me with a broad smile and open arms.

"So, how did you do, Melissa? Do you think you passed?" Jesse asked.

"I can only hope." I reply, noticing then that their arms are quite empty. "Where's the food?"

"I'm hoping the others are bringing it in because I'm starving," Josh replies. He really is no help at all. None of them are.

Hoping to be of some kind of assistance since I technically took the day off work, I sprint outside to see if

Joni, Sam, Oliver, and the rest of the crew need any help. I spy Joni first, climbing out of one of the rental vans with two plastic sacks full of takeout Thai food.

"Hey, do you need any help?" I ask.

"Wow, Mel, how nice of you to offer. You know what would also be nice? If my brother and his band of goonies actually lifted a finger to help out once in a while!" Joni huffs. Clearly, this has not been her day either. I'll give her one of my Snickers later.

"Where are Sam and Oliver?"

"I'm still back here," Oliver calls from inside the van. "And I've got the drinks."

"What about Sam?"

"He went in with the rest of the Peanut Gallery," Joni says.

"Really? I didn't see him," I say. Is it possible he's already upstairs? Maybe we crossed paths and I didn't even realize it.

Shrugging it off, I take one of the plastic sacks from Joni and head back to the hotel. I figure Oliver will be more than happy to help her out. Hey, I may have struck out on love, but I'm really hoping that he still has a shot.

I'm just about at the door when a voice I know too well catches my ear. It's Sam. And I think he's in the alley.

"Look, I'm sorry. I don't know how it got this far," he's saying.

"I know, and I'm not blaming you," a new voice, distinctly female, replies. "But I've tried quelling the rumors myself and it's not working. I need you to say something."

Chloe Conley.

"I will."

"Listen Sam, I want you to know I think you're a really good guy. And I know that people are always going to talk. A lot of that is my doing after what happened with Josh last year. But I really need all of this to stop. Not just for me, but for my fans. They matter more to me than anything, and I can't stand seeing them attacked for something that has nothing to do with them. Or me, for that matter."

"I know. And again, I'm sorry. A lot of things were taken out of context."

"It happens," Chloe says. "Well listen, I've got to go. I have a date tonight. But it was good to see you again."

"You too, Chloe," Sam replies.

I don't hear the rest of their goodbye. I'm too busy scurrying back to the hotel as fast as my feet can carry me. I don't want either one of them, especially Sam, to catch me spying on them. It's difficult to run, however, when your heart is already beating a million miles a minute.

What just happened? Did Chloe and Sam break up? Or were they never actually together? From what it sounded like, she doesn't feel the same way and she never did. She's even going on date with someone else tonight. I don't want to feel happy about this, you know, for Sam's sake, but I'm ashamed to admit that I suddenly like Chloe Conley a lot more than I did about ten minutes ago.

But Sam! What about him? He must be heartbroken. Or at least let down. No matter how much I wanted this (and I really, really wanted it), I can't be happy knowing that it's come at his expense. Knowing that he's hurting is, in a way, even worse than knowing that he liked someone else.

I kind of figured I wasn't going to win this one, but I never imagined it was a lose-lose situation no matter the outcome. For him as much as me.

Chapter Nineteen

"And won't you think of me
If you're feeling lonely
And you don't know where to run
And won't you think of me
When the night is falling
I want to help you find the sun
Won't you think of me
Because I'll be thinking of you..."

Song: "Think of Me"
Artist: The Kind of September
From the Album: *17 Times Over*

Once, after the guys' second album came out, I was scrolling through posts on Twitter. Most of the comments were positive, but there was one remark that stood out to me.

How can Sam Morneau or any of #TKOS sing about being lonely or feeling sad? They could literally have anyone they wanted.

At first, I kind of thought they had a point. Most of the time, it seems like the guys have conquered the world. They're rich, famous, popular, handsome, and yeah, could probably have any single person that they want, just because they're The Kind of September. And that's where things get complicated.

The guys have always agreed that it's strange meeting someone new, because they can never be sure that they like them for who they really are. It sounds so cliché, I know, but that age-old saying is true. It is lonely at the top.

They're young, they have their whole lives ahead of them and the entire world to explore, but at the end of the day, we all look forward to having someone to love. We all wonder who will share our lives. The guys are the same way. They want to feel loved and accepted, and sometimes, they struggle with it. Just like everybody else.

That's why I'm worried for Sam tonight. He rarely gets emotional or truly upset about anything. He hates for anyone to know that something is bothering him. He'd rather brush it off with a laugh or a smile. But I have a terrible feeling that what happened tonight with Chloe will get to him. Not because he was desperately in love with her, but because of the way he sounded when he was apologizing to her. He sounded so repentant, like he had actually done something wrong.

I'm even more concerned because we've had dinner up here in Josh, Jesse, and Oliver's room for almost twenty minutes and he still hasn't shown up. Sam doesn't miss meals. It just doesn't happen. And I know I'm not going to be able to eat until I know that he's okay.

As if he's read my thoughts, Josh asks, "Where the hell is Sam, anyway? Did he miss the memo that we have Thai up here?"

"Doubtful, since he was with us when we got it," Oliver says.

"I'll go find him," I announce. I don't think anyone is surprised. Or eager to join me, for that matter. Food is probably way too high up on their priority lists.

Setting my untouched plate of pad thai and spring rolls aside, I leave the guys' room and head a mere two doors down to Sam and Cory's room. I knock on the door, hoping that he'll answer. He probably will. Sam isn't the kind of person who shuts his friends out, even when he wants to be alone.

Sure enough, he answers within seconds. He's already dressed in his baggy tank top and pajama pants and he's munching on a mouthful of potato chips. I guess that means that if he is upset about Chloe, he's not upset about it enough to not eat. That's a good sign.

"Hey," I greet him. "You okay?"

"Yep. I'm good," he replies. At first, I wonder why he's trying to act like there's nothing going on. Then I remember that he doesn't know that I overheard what happened between him and Chloe.

"Why aren't you at dinner?"

He shrugs. "Not really in the mood for Thai."

"Oh. Okay." I'm not sure how to go about any of this, so I just keep talking. "Do you want some company?"

"As long as you don't have a hidden camera designed to locate my secret stash," he replies with a grin.

"Oh, darn. You just thwarted my evil plan."

"I know you too well," he says with a wink.

I make my way inside, astonished by the mess they've already managed to make inside the room. Or should I say the mess that Sam has already managed to make. Cory's side of the room is spotless, as it should be, considering we've only been here about eight hours.

"Did your suitcase accidentally explode?" I ask Sam.

"What? This is tidy," he claims.

"You are so lucky you're cute," I tell him. Usually, that would get a quick smile out of him, maybe even a bit of a blush. But he doesn't even blink.

"Yeah, well, I'm not sure that will do anything for me either," he remarks, dropping down onto his bed.

"What does that mean?" I ask, taking a seat next to him.

"Nothing, nothing," he replies with a wave of his hand. "I'm just saying stuff."

"Does it have something to do with Chloe?" I ask without even thinking as he turns curious albeit dreamy blue eyes on me.

And now he knows that I was spying on him. Oh well. He was going to figure it out eventually. I might as well come out and admit it.

"Why do you say that?" he asks.

"Because I'm your best friend and I can read your mind," I tell him. "That, or I may have overheard you talking to her in the alley when I went out to help bring the food in." He looks like he doesn't know how to respond, so I quickly apologize. "I'm sorry. I didn't mean to listen. I heard you talking and I didn't know what to do and I wanted to know that you were okay and... I'm so sorry."

"Don't be sorry. I'm not mad at you," he assures me.

"Are you sure? Because I might be mad at me." I mean, most normal people would be mad, right? I just openly admitted to eavesdropping on a very personal conversation. But Sam doesn't seem to care.

"I could never be mad at you, Mel. You know that."

Why? Why did he have go and say those totally wonderful and adorable words? See, this is the kind of thing that makes it so hard for me to not love him. Not to mention the fact that his hair is all messy and I've got a really great view of the tattoos on his chest thanks to the tank top that he's wearing and -

Oh my God! What am I thinking? My friend just had his heart broken in a Los Angeles alleyway and here I am trying to sneak a peek at his almost-naked torso!

"So," I clear my throat, hoping he doesn't realize just how close I came to gawking at his sexy tattoos. "Are you okay?"

"Yeah, I'm fine," he says, but his words sound off, almost automatic.

"Are you really okay?" I press, but he doesn't respond. It's only then that I realize just how much this whole situation really is bothering him. "I'm sorry, Sam. I know you really liked her."

"That's the thing, Mel. I didn't like her."

"What?" What does he mean he didn't like her? True, he never outright said that it was her that he liked, but there was obviously something there to make the entire world think that they were in love. "Well, that's a good thing, isn't it? If you didn't like her, then why worry about what she said?"

"I have a feeling you didn't hear the entire conversation," Sam tells me. "She told me that dating me, even rumors about dating me, were terrible for her career and her image. She said she's never had so much hatred directed at her, that her reps were overwhelmed with media outlets wondering if she knew about my quote-unquote reputation as a womanizer and all-around douchebag."

"What?" At first, I can't believe what I'm hearing. Then I wonder why. I've always known that the media likes to portray Sam as the heartbreaker of the group. I guess I'm just surprised that Chloe would hold that against him.

"I can't blame her. I wouldn't want to be known for dating a Kelli Barnett or a Tara Meeks."

"But Sam, you are so much better than those girls."

"Not according to the media. Even if they did portray me in a decent light, so many of the fans care so much about who I date that they'd probably harass anyone I supposedly was with if they didn't feel like she was good enough for me."

"Well, I guess it's nice that they're protective," I offer tentatively. Sam shakes his head and manages a chuckle, but I know this is still bothering him. "Sam, you've known for a long time that the media likes to spread lies about you and that the fans can be a little... rabid." Again, the small laugh. The sound makes my heart skip. "Why is it getting to you now?"

"It's gotten to me long before this, but I've always been able to shrug it off, reminding myself how fortunate I am to be here, and how all the good things in my life so far outweigh the bad that I shouldn't even be permitted to dwell. But I think hearing Chloe say that the idea of dating me was bad for her career... it kind of made me realize that I'd be toxic for any girl, not just a celebrity with an image to maintain."

"Sam..." The look on his face, the sadness in his voice, is breaking my heart all over again. "You can't think that."

"It doesn't matter what I think. It's true. It doesn't matter who I date, or who I'm even seen with. Assumptions are going to be made, rumors are going to fly, online abuse is going to skyrocket, and I just couldn't let anyone go through that, especially someone I really care about."

"Sam, I know it seems like that now, but if a girl loves you, if she really loves you, that stuff won't matter. I mean, it probably won't be fun, but if having to endure a little gossip is the price to pay to be with you, I think any girl would gladly pay that price. They'd probably be willing to pay more."

By now, I'm feeling dizzy and lightheaded. Not because my heart is pounding so fast I can barely breathe, but because my emotions are running so high and so raw that I'm afraid, if I'm not careful, they might consume what little rationality I possess. But I can't seem to stop the words from tumbling out of my mouth. I need Sam to know how much he means, not just to me, but to so many people around the world.

"But they shouldn't have to," Sam argues with me. "No one should have to pay any price to be with someone. I'm not worth that."

"Sam, how can you say that? You are so worth it," I insist, looking him square in the eye. "You're worth everything."

And that's when I kiss him.

Trust me, I had no idea this was coming. This is not a premeditated act. It's barely even a conscious one, and it's over before I even realize that it's happened. I don't have time to think about how soft his lips were beneath mine, or the fact that I could feel his breath on my face, or that his hand slipped over to mine before I pull away, totally and completely mortified.

Oh my God. Oh my God, what have I done?

If the look on his face is any indication, he's feeling about the same way.

I know I say this a lot, but this time, my life is *really* over.

"Oh my God," I gasp. "Oh my God, I am so sorry. Sam, I - I don't know why I did that. I'm so sorry. Please, forget that happened." Trembling all over, I leap to my feet and stumble across the mess of scattered clothes and trash to the door, all the while rambling off pathetic apologies over and over again. "Really, I don't know what got into me. You just looked so sad and I wanted to make you feel better, and I know I shouldn't have, but I really wasn't thinking."

All the while, Sam looks like he's doing some quick consideration. His eyebrows are furrowed and his lips are still parted, almost like they're frozen in place by my kiss. I don't know if that's a good thing or a bad thing, so I keep talking. It comes pretty naturally, especially since he's suddenly clammed up like... well, a *clam*.

"Anyway, I really probably should get going. I hope you're not mad and I really hope that this isn't going to make things weird between us, because you're my best friend and -"

Before I can say another word, however, Sam has crossed the room in just a few long-legged strides. He takes his fingers and brushes my loose strands of hair away from my eyes, cupping my face in his hands. He presses his slim body up against mine and he looks at me with those eyes that I've known and loved my entire life.

And that's when he kisses me.

Chapter Twenty

"Her hand was never his to hold
Her love is yours, or so I'm told
So tell me what are you waiting for?
Don't just stand there
She's waiting for you
To take back her heart..."

Song: "Take Back Her Heart"
Artist: The Kind of September
From the Album: *The Kind of September*

The first time Sam kissed me, we were ten years old. Our families were having lunch down at West Bluffs Picnic Area. It was a beautiful summer day. The sea and the sky were shimmering shades of blue, the grass was green, and we had a perfect view of the Golden Gate Bridge. As usual, Sam and I had run off, seeking adventure. Or maybe, even then, we just wanted to be with each other. Either way, we ended up running down the beach toward the pier.

The water was a little cold for swimming, but not too cold to keep us from splashing around with our bare feet. Despite the chill, we both ended up drenched from head to toe and covered in sand.

I know, it really doesn't sound very romantic. In fact, there was absolutely nothing romantic about it. I can't really even remember how it even came up. It was kind of just one of those kid moments. We were searching for sea glass when we spotted a young couple running into the ocean and laughing. The guy grabbed the girl by the waist and twirled her around. Then she wrapped her arms around his neck and kissed him.

"Have you ever kissed anyone?" Sam asked.

"No."

"It looks like it'd be weird." Typical boy comment.

"Yeah," I agreed, wanting to sound cool, like I really didn't care one way or another. But I was ten years old, old enough to qualify as a pre-teen. I'd be lying if I said I hadn't thought about kissing before.

Sam kicked around in the sand for a few more moments before he asked, "Would you kiss me?"

I stared at him, trying to figure out if he was joking or not. Once I realized that he wasn't, I said, "Okay." That was seriously all it took. If my parents had overheard that conversation, they'd probably be just a tad bit concerned that their eldest daughter was so compliant at such a young age.

I still remember everything about that first kiss. He closed his eyes, but I kept mine open at the last millisecond, certain that I was somehow going to mess it up. But I didn't. The kiss was quick and a little abrasive, as kid kisses tend to be, but it was still the most exciting moment of my life up until that point.

After it ended, we never spoke of it again. To anyone. I don't know why, really. I guess for the same reason I never told him how I really feel about it. Because I didn't want to ruin what we had.

It's kind of weird when you think about it: the idea that telling someone that you love them, that you really care about them, will somehow ruin a relationship. I guess it happens, especially if someone doesn't reciprocate, but doesn't everyone want to be told that they're loved? That they're special to someone? How can that be a bad thing? But in my mind, it was.

For the record, I don't think that anymore.

❀♫✿

Of all the scenarios that I imagined involving Sam kissing me, this is one that I only halfway expected. Yeah, I kind of thought that it might happen while we were alone in his hotel room. I mean, we are alone in there a lot. But I always kind of expected it to be a shy kiss, sort of bashful, maybe a little reluctant.

This kiss is none of the above.

It's the kind of kiss you see in movies. It's confident and passionate and sexy. It's so many things that my mind actually goes blank, having short-circuited trying to keep up with all these new sensations.

SAM is kissing me. Sam is KISSING me. Sam is kissing ME.

After he pulls away, we stare at each other for a few moments. He looks about as dazed and incoherent as I feel.

"Wow," is all I can manage.

He just grins and kisses me again, which I am totally okay with.

This time I try to think less. I'm not an experienced kisser, by any means, so I'm kind of terrified that I'll somehow screw this up. Sam, on the other hand, isn't concerned at all. Like most everything else in the world, kissing just seems to come naturally to him. That, or he's had a lot more practice than I have. We'll go with the first theory.

Unlike most kisses I've seen and experienced, where the guy wraps his arm around the girl's waist, Sam is content keeping his hands close to my face. I don't mind, not in the least. The way he's delicately touching my skin and running fingers through my hair, it feels like he cherishes me, like I'm something precious. His touch alone is enough to make me weak at the knees.

When we break apart again, he looks at me and says, "You know, if I didn't know better... I'd think you liked me."

And for some reason, I laugh. Maybe it's because when you've just been kissed by the guy you love, everything is so perfect that you can't help but laugh. Or maybe I do think he's that funny, even though, let's be honest, he's really not. I don't think he was even trying. Either way, I'm laughing. And then he starts laughing.

"Why - Why is this so funny?" he asks.

"I don't know," I somehow manage to say between laughs. "It's ridiculous."

"It is. But haven't we always been kind of ridiculous?"

"Yeah, kind of," I acknowledge. Then I wrap my arms around his neck and kiss him again.

"No, seriously," he asks after the kiss ends. "Did you plan this?"

"I'm flattered that you think I'm that crafty," I reply. "I had no idea this was going to happen. I mean, yeah, I may have thought about before... you know, from time to time." And now I'm blushing. Hard.

"Why didn't you tell me?" Sam asks.

"Because I didn't think you felt the same way."

"Mel." He takes both of my hands in his. "I've never known how to feel about you. Or I guess I've never known how you wanted me to feel."

"What do you mean?"

"I mean, I was in love with you all throughout high school."

"You - I - What?" Oh, so eloquent. "Why didn't you ever ask me out?"

He shrugs. "One day I was waiting for you at your locker, and I overheard you and a few other girls talking. You were insisting that you and I were just friends, no romantic feelings whatsoever."

I think I know what day he's talking about. It was right around Homecoming our junior year and my friends were all convinced that Sam and I were dating and that we'd be going together. I knew that if I let my friends know I liked him then one of them would go running off to Sam, telling him to ask me to the dance, so I swore up and down that our relationship was strictly platonic. I remember that day specifically because it was the same day he asked Cameron Griffith out.

"I had no idea you heard that," I tell him.

"I guess you're not the only one who eavesdrops," he says with a nudge and a grin. "Anyway, I figured I'd rather have you as a friend than nothing at all, so I moved on. Or I tried to." He looks me in the eye. "You're kind of hard to get over, Mel."

By now, my heart is fluttering so quickly that I'm certain I'll faint. I think about sticking my head between my knees, but I can't think of anything that could possibly be less romantic after the guy of my dreams tells me that he's in love with me.

"I can't believe I was so stupid," I mutter.

"It was high school. We were all stupid. Besides, I did the same thing the other night when I told Courtney and Tara that there was someone else."

"You mean there isn't?" I ask.

"You still thought there was?" he laughs.

Oh, right. Maybe not.

"Well, you sounded very adamant," I tell him.

"That's because I didn't want Tara pulling that same stunt with you and me that she did with you and Oliver."

"What?"

Sam sighs, and for the first time since the kiss, he lets me go. Then, he meanders back to the bed and sits down, running a hand through his hair. I follow quietly and sit down next to him.

"I knew that if either Tara or Courtney thought, even for a second, that there was something going on between us, that would be it. They'd spread it around on Twitter and Facebook and every other site that we were dating, or worse, that I'd stolen you from Oliver, just like I stole Chloe from Josh. And I couldn't let that happen to you."

"You were trying to protect me." It all makes sense.

"In a really weird, twisted way, yeah," he says, offering up a wry half-smile.

"So wait, why were you so happy when everyone thought I was dating Oliver?"

"I guess I wasn't happy so much as, well, a little encouraged," he explained. "I thought that since everyone seemed okay with you dating Oliver, then maybe they'd be okay with you dating me. I thought, maybe since you're a girl that the fans already know and love, it wouldn't be that big a deal. But now..."

"Now what?"

"Now I'm afraid that even though people like you, your reputation is still going to be compromised if we..." He trails off again.

"If we...?"

"You know." And suddenly, just like that, he's bashful. "If we were together."

"You mean if I was your girlfriend?" I ask, feeling the color gathering in my cheeks as well. With an impish gleam in his eye, he leans forward and kisses me swiftly in response. I swear, if we keep this up, we are never going to leave this room.

Not that that would be a bad thing.

Once I'm able to form a coherent thought, I tell him, "Sam, I meant what I said earlier. I don't care what anyone thinks or says about me."

"Yes, you do. And I do, too. To put you through even a fraction of what Chloe went through in the last few days... I don't think I could live with myself."

"And I love you for that," I say. "But it doesn't matter to me. It doesn't matter what anyone says or thinks or does. Yeah, it will probably be hard some of the time, and yeah, words and rumors can be just as hurtful as sticks and stones, but all of that is irrelevant. Because in the end, I know I'm always going to choose you. If you want me to."

Again, he reaches out, brushes my hair back behind my ears, and looks me in the eye.

"I've always wanted you to, Mel," he murmurs.

And again, he kisses me.

✽♪♪✽

Kissing Sam is addictive. I mean, I kind of knew it would be. But I didn't expect it to feel so natural, like we were designed for each other. I also didn't anticipate how easy it would be for us to transition from Friends to More-Than-Friends. Maybe because we've both secretly been there all along.

"You know," he says in between kisses, "the others are probably wondering where we are."

The others? What others? We have others?

Oh, right. Our friends. Joni and Josh and all them. They exist too.

But I bet they don't kiss like this.

"Do you want to head back?" I ask him.

"No," he replies, kissing me beneath my ear. "But I also really don't want them to come looking for us."

"True," I acknowledge. "So what do we tell them?"

"What do you think?"

Why is he asking me? I can barely string two words together, let alone make any sort of critical decisions regarding our relationship and how to move forward with it.

"I'm kind of drawing a blank on this one," I admit to him, running a few fingers through his thick, dark blond locks.

"So am I," he replies.

"I mean... I guess we don't have to tell them anything," I say. "They know that we have a weird relationship anyway. They're constantly reminding us of it."

"I think they kind of know that I like you," Sam confesses.

"I was convinced they knew that *I* like *you*."

"Maybe they all knew before we did."

"If we don't tell them we've made it official, or whatever this is, then it might be easier to keep a low profile with the fans and the media," I ponder out loud.

"Is that what you want?"

"I just want you. You're all I've ever wanted," I tell him. "But I do know that all the rumors get to you."

"It's not about me. I can take care of myself. It's about you."

"I know. So maybe, just for now, it would be easier if we didn't tell anyone. That way, we can go on tour and not have a million eyes and cameras and questions following us everywhere we go. We can just enjoy the tour."

"And make out backstage," he grins and presses his lips to my cheek. "You know, I've always wanted to do that."

"What? Make out backstage?"

"Yeah. Isn't that what all the greats do?"

"I have no idea," I laugh. Then I pull him back into another kiss.

Chapter Twenty-One

"And I love that look in your eyes
When you tell me that you love me
And that smile on your lips
When you say that I'm the only one
Now it's you and me girl
It's you and me forever
And I'm never gonna let you go..."

Song: "Forever"
Artist: The Kind of September
From the Album: *Meet Me on the Midway*

Here's the thing about being in a relationship with the guy you've been in love with for practically your entire life. It's really hard to keep it a secret. Even if you don't come out and say it, you suddenly give off this ridiculously happy glow that your friends that really, really know you couldn't miss even if they tried. I'm pretty sure even a complete stranger could count the stars in my eyes.

It was probably the singing that gave me away. Unlike Sam, who likes to sing and radiates this almost insane sense of joy and life on a regular basis, I'm not one to hum or whistle or anything of the sort. But in the days following my evening with Sam, I can't stop singing. Joni finally confronts me about it while the guys are preparing for their final interview on a talk show that will air later tonight.

"Okay, what is going on with you?" she demands.

"What do you mean?" That sounded so false. Hopefully she won't notice.

"I mean you can't stop smiling. You're like a puppy with a new squeaky toy."

"That's an interesting simile," I remark.

"You know what I mean. Something is going on. So spill."

"Well, I found out that I passed my exams."

"Oh please, you've never cared *that* much about schoolwork." She's got me there.

"I guess I'm just really happy for the guys," I tell her.

And why wouldn't I be? We just found out that their album shot to the number one spot in the charts in almost record time, not to mention they released the "Meet Me on the Midway" video last night at midnight. Sam and I spent the first part of the evening with the rest of the group, but then, claiming exhaustion, we excused ourselves and snuck back to his room for a more private celebration.

It was probably one of the best nights of my life. These past few nights with Sam have *all* been the best nights of my life. And I imagine they're only going to get better once we're back home.

Oh! That's another reason to be happy! We're going home today.

"I'm also super excited about having some time off," I add, hoping I don't sound like I'm trying too hard.

"Oh God, me too," Joni sighs. "One last interview for the guys and then we are out of here. I swear to you, I'm going to sleep for like, two days."

"I'm going to sleep for like, two weeks," I say. Except for when I'm making out with Sam. Or eating. I'll definitely wake up for food. Other than that, there will be a lot of relaxing going on this holiday season.

Alas, we've still got a few more hours to go before that blessed flight home to San Francisco.

About half an hour before they're scheduled to go on, Sam emerges from the dressing room, nonchalantly takes my hand, and leads me to an empty stairwell inside the studio.

"Hi." He smiles at me.

"Hi," I respond, taking his shirt in my hands and pulling him closer to me. "Don't you look handsome." He does, too. His hair is parted off to the side and styled to perfection and he's wearing dark jeans and a blue button-down shirt.

"Oh, stop." He pretends to be embarrassed. Then he says, "Okay, you can keep going."

I laugh and kiss him. I'm not sure if you've ever kissed a guy in a place you're really not supposed to be, but let me tell you, it is exhilarating. Sam must feel it too, because he wraps his arms around my waist and lifts me right up off the ground. I'm glad my mouth is preoccupied, otherwise I probably would have shrieked and ruined the whole moment. And possibly our whole secret relationship as well.

"I can't wait to get home," he murmurs. "No rehearsals, no interviews, no god-awful hair and make-up. Just you and me. And maybe a movie night here and there."

"How about an evening stroll down by the pier?" I ask.

"Or a midnight drive across the Golden Gate Bridge?"

It's almost too much to look forward to. There's nothing I can do except wrap my arms back around Sam's neck and kiss him again.

One more interview, I tell myself. *One more interview and then we all go home. One more interview and then he's all mine.*

"You know, Joni was asking me why I was so happy earlier," I tell him, twirling a stray lock of his hair.

"Oh yeah?" he grins. "What did you tell her?"

"Something about your album going to number one and your music video being all good and stuff, I don't really remember."

"It's the little things," he comments.

"Exactly."

I'm about ready to lean in and kiss him yet again when he asks me, "So uh, do you think Oliver's ever going to tell her how he feels?"

And just like that, the spell is broken.

"You know about that?"

"We all do. That was another reason I was kind of amused when the world thought Meliver was a thing."

"Aw, poor Oliver."

"Poor Oliver? I was the one who had to watch the Internet pair up the girl I like with one of my bandmates."

"Oh yeah, you were utterly devastated."

"I was. On the inside."

"Oh, whatever."

We make out for about five more minutes before he regretfully has to meet up with the rest of the guys for the interview. I linger in the stairwell for a few additional minutes, just in case someone happened to see him emerge. I wouldn't want anyone to think we were doing exactly what we were actually doing. Thankfully, we both emerge from the stairwell with our dignity and reputations (or what remains of them anyway) intact.

❀♪❀

"Welcome, to the show gentlemen," renowned television talk-show host Jack Landon greets the guys once they've ambled onstage.

"Thanks, Jack. It's great to be here," Josh smiles.

"Now, you've just released your third album, *Meet Me on the Midway*, which has soared to the top of the charts in no time flat. How do you celebrate something like that?"

"Sleep, mostly," Sam quips. The audience laughs. More than a few girls catcall.

"I think we're all looking forward to having some time off," Jesse says.

Beside me, someone tries to stifle a whimper. I don't have to look to know it's Tara. Who has decided to grace us with her presence. Again.

Seriously, what is she doing here? I thought she was still in New York. Apparently not.

"Shh," Joni shushes her.

"I'm sorry, I'm just - " she fans her face, attempting to dry tears I'm not sure are even there. "I'm just going to miss him so much. I can't believe it will be a whole month before I get to see him again."

"Yeah, well, life is hard," Joni mutters under her breath.

"Oliver, how about you?" Jack asks. "Are you flying back home to London?"

"Yeah, actually. My parents live here, but we fly back every year to see my grandparents."

"I bet they're pretty proud of you."

"All of our families are," Oliver says.

"Now Sam. There have been some interesting reports flying around about your love life lately," Jack says.

"Aren't there always?" Sam asks, eliciting another laugh from the audience. "I can tell you that I've yet to hear a rumor that's true."

"So, you're not seeing Chloe Conley right now? Because I've got to tell you, that girl is gorgeous. I mean, you'd pretty much make the perfect power couple."

"Chloe's a friend. But that's all," Sam smiles with that easy grace of his that I've secretly always envied. He's so good at presenting himself. He always knows exactly what do say. I'd kill for that kind of confidence.

"Is there someone else?" Jack presses.

"Let's just say everything is as it should be," Sam answers.

"I have no idea what that means," Jack says.

"Then you're on the same page as everyone else," Cory jokes.

"Now Cory, you're still with your lady friend, am I correct?"

"Yes, you are correct," Cory grins like a fool. The audience cheers and whistles. It kind of seems like a programmed response by now. But Tara soaks it up anyway.

"Any romantic plans for the holidays?"

"Still working on it," Cory replies. I guess that means he hasn't given up on the idea of having Tara come stay with them for a few days. Hopefully, Mrs. Foreman is still holding fast.

"I hear you, I hear you. So what's next for you guys? After the holidays are over?"

"The tour," Josh replies.

"Yeah, we go into rehearsals early January and then we're on the road for ten months," Oliver says.

"That sounds like a blast," Jack says.

"It's going to be great. The best tour yet," Sam tells him. By now, the fans are going wild. They are clearly more excited about the tour than Cory and Tara's love life. Honestly, I really can't blame them.

"Well, I wish you guys all the best and congratulations on all your success," Jack tells them.

The guys all thank him. And then it's over.

It's time to go home.

❀♫♪❀

Packing up at the end of the season is always stressful, just because everyone has So. Much. Stuff. It's the same thing every year. If we're not scavenging the hotel for every last item in our possession, we're double and triple checking our luggage to make sure that even if something has disappeared, it isn't anything important. Then, without fail, someone will remember something they left in the lobby or in the room and then we'll have to go back to the front desk, retrieve the key, and hike all the way back up to the room for whatever's been left behind if for no other reason than to ensure it doesn't end up on eBay.

Okay, there are elevators so we don't actually have to hike, but you get what I'm saying.

Every year we all vow that we're going to pack and travel light, but somehow, it hasn't happened yet. Maybe next year. This year, it's the same old song and dance of scrambling around for everything in order to make our flight. And let me tell you, we're cutting it kind of close.

It didn't help that Tara was here earlier, distracting Cory and encouraging the rest of the guys not to worry about being on time and that they were so famous and so important that they could call the airline and demand the plane wait for them and so on and so forth. I may not have made this clear, but I am really not going to miss her at all. Thankfully, she wasn't around when Joni discovered one of Sam's discarded shirts underneath my bed.

I was fully prepared to lie through my teeth about how the shirt came to be there, but strangely, she didn't ask, nor did she seem all that surprised by it at all. I guess that just goes to show how weird people think our relationship actually is. Or maybe she was too stressed about us potentially being late to really care all that much. Whatever the reason, our secret is still ours.

For now.

Within fifteen minutes, Joni and I are locking up our room and heading down to the lobby to check out. If the guys are down there, they're probably already waiting for us in the vans. Security likes to get them in and out of buildings with as little fuss as possible.

Once we check out and get our luggage loaded into the vans, Josh pokes his head out one of the windows.

"Hey, is Jesse with you?" he asks.

"No. He's not with you?" I ask.

"Haven't seen him since he brought his bags down," Josh replies. "Do you think one of you could go look for him? He's not answering his phone"

Given Joni's still-rocky relationship with Jesse, I volunteer. Though to be honest, I have no idea where to start looking. This hotel is huge. There are literally a hundred places he could be.

I stop by the front desk first and ask the guy working there if he's seen "Jesse from The Kind of September" wandering around anywhere. He tells me that he hasn't, but mentions that one key card is still unaccounted for.

Great. That means Jesse is still up in his hotel room, probably looking for his phone charger or something. His phone is probably dead and that's why no one can get a hold of him and now we're going to miss our flight because he can't keep up with things.

With few other options, I ride the elevator back up to our suites on the twelfth floor. As I walk down the hall, I debate whether I should give him a lecture or just wait and let Joni do the honors. She's a lot better at lectures than I am, but I really, really want to go home.

The door to his room is still ajar, so I take the liberty of letting myself in.

"Jesse, what are you doing? We need to - "

But I'm stopped dead in my tracks. Because I'm not looking at Jesse. I'm looking at Jesse and someone else.

Jesse and a tall, beautiful, blonde someone.

Jesse and Tara.

Kissing.

Can't get enough of The Kind of September?

Please turn this page for a preview of the second book in the
Boy Band series

Backstage

Backstage

If there's one thing I've learned in my almost twenty-one years, it's that life after Happily Ever After is just as complicated and confusing, if not more so, than life before it. I really didn't think it would be, and to be honest, I blame that on Hollywood. All those romance movies would have you believe that once you find that one perfect guy, everything else just magically falls into place.

The real problem with stories like that is that they end before the Ever After part actually begins. The couple finally declares their love for one another and once they kiss, the credits roll. You never see them go back to living their regular lives now that they've made this commitment to one another. Do they go out on lunch dates? Do they take turns folding the laundry or argue over what they need to buy at the grocery store?

Granted, my own Happily Ever After is a little out of the ordinary. For one thing, the only person in the world who knows I'm dating Sam Morneau is his mom, Laurel, and that's because he's never been able to keep a secret from her. For another, we've been best friends practically our entire lives, so it's not like we've had to get used to each other's quirks or eccentricities. And finally, Sam is an internationally acclaimed superstar, which is awesome, but you know, also kind of strange.

Don't get me wrong. I'm used to the idea of Sam being famous. After all, The Kind of September has been one of the most popular bands on the planet for over two years. Their third album, *Meet Me on the Midway*, went platinum within weeks of its release, and I couldn't be more thrilled for them. I don't think any of our friends or families could.

But the fact still stands that my relationship with him will never be normal. And that's fine. I love Sam. I've been in love with him since before I knew what it meant to really be in love. Neither the nature nor normalcy of our relationship matters to me as long as I'm with him. And I think he feels the same way about me. It would be nice if we could actually go out on dates though. *Real* dates. Sure, we can go out for a casual coffee date or hang out as friends at Fisherman's Wharf. But we can't dress up and have dinner at a romantic restaurant or hold hands and watch the sun set out on the pier. Instead, we spend most of our date nights locked up in one of our rooms. Well actually, Laurel never lets us close the door. It doesn't matter that he's twenty years old and one of the most famous people on the planet. Sam will always be her baby boy. It's sweet.

My mom, on the other hand, has no idea that Sam and I are secretly dating. No one in my family does. That's why, when we meet up at my place, my mom has no problem with us closing the door. We've been sneaking up to my room and locking the door since we were twelve years old. Of course, back then, we were swapping Pokémon cards and playing video games on my hand-me-down Play Station, so she really had no reason to be suspicious.

He's actually coming over tonight, but not for a date night. Christmas is only a week away so Sam, Cory, Joni, and I decided to celebrate a little early with a holiday movie night. We would have invited the rest of the guys but Josh and his family are in Hawaii for a tropical Christmas, Oliver and his family are back home in England, and Jesse... well, I just really didn't want to invite Jesse. Joni didn't either, but not for the same reason.

Joni doesn't want Jesse around because he's her ex-boyfriend and even though she swears up and down that she has no problem with him, I think she's still hurt over the fact that he broke up with her. I don't want him around because about three weeks ago, on our very last day in Los Angeles, I walked in on him making out with Cory's supermodel girlfriend, Tara.

Excuse me when I say this but OH MY GOD. Really, Jesse? *Really*? There are hundreds of thousands of single girls all over the world who would date him in a heartbeat, but no. He just had to go for someone else's girlfriend. His best friend's girlfriend. *His ex-girlfriend's twin brother's girlfriend.*

I can't handle this. I really can't.

The worst part wasn't even walking in and catching them. It was the way they reacted to me catching them. I have never been more embarrassed in my life, which is sort of weird considering that I wasn't the one who'd just been caught in an affair which had apparently been going on for three weeks. Three weeks! Cory and Tara haven't even been together for two months and she's already been seeing Jesse behind his back for *three weeks*?

Anyway, once they realized I was standing there, they both started freaking out. Jesse ran and slammed the door shut behind me which, I'm not going to lie to you, startled me a lot more than it should have. Tara began rattling off excuses about how she'd never meant to hurt Cory and how she loved him so much but she loved Jesse too and she just didn't know what to do.

"It's not like I could help it, you know? I mean, I tried, because Cory is such a good guy. But you know how when you feel something for someone? And Jesse couldn't help it, either. There's just that spark. I can't explain it. You won't tell anyone, will you?"

"Uhh..." At that point, I really didn't know what to say. I mean, what do you say in that situation? *Bad Tara! You can't kiss Jesse! You're dating Cory!* But I couldn't even manage that. I was too shocked to form a coherent thought.

I guess Jesse could tell that I was kind of short-circuiting, because he stepped in front of me and placed both hands on my shoulders.

"Melissa," he said in an oddly calm and authoritative voice. "Listen to me. Don't tell anyone about this, okay?"

"I can't - I don't -"

"I know. Just hear me out. Look, we know this is wrong. I hate sneaking around behind Cory's back. But it's like Tara said. We just can't help it. This isn't something that we planned. It just happened. But listen, we're not making any hasty decisions. We're just trying to figure out where this is all going."

"You're trying to figure out where it's *going*?!" I asked, not believing a word that he'd just said. "Jesse, that's what single people say."

"I am single."

"Yeah, but *she's* not!" I pointed at Tara.

"Mel, please, *please* don't tell anyone about this. *Please*, it would ruin everything." Tara was so upset, she sounded like she was about to cry. But to be honest, I didn't feel all that sorry for her. Yeah, it would ruin everything for her. It would ruin her relationship with Cory, her one claim to fame. Although, to be honest, she'd be a lot more famous if she and

Jesse got caught. The tabloids would have a field day. Not to mention all the social media fame that would come with it. It's weird, but in the entertainment industry, sometimes scandal is the best thing that can happen to a person.

But apparently, Tara isn't ready for *that* kind of fame yet, since she kept blubbering on and on about how she would do anything I wanted as long as I didn't tell anyone.

Jesse, who was still pretty level-headed, all things considered, went on to list all the other reasons, besides Tara's precious reputation, why I shouldn't tell anyone, the first and foremost of those reasons being the new album. It had only just been released and was doing so well. Any sort of bad press whatsoever might jeopardize the whole group.

I tried arguing back that a secret affair with his bandmate's girlfriend could jeopardize the group also, but he was already on to reminding me about the upcoming world tour and how if word got out about an affair, they'd be letting fans all over the world down and then people might not come to the shows and how it might ruin the tour for Cory and a whole bunch of other nonsense.

Again, I tried to reiterate that this was all very easily avoidable if they just called off the relationship, but I knew the moment I suggested it that it wasn't going to happen. Both Jesse and Tara *really* wanted to keep on seeing each other. And as far as I know, they still are.

I thought that my romance with Sam was the hardest secret I'd ever have to keep. This is so much worse though, because for the first time in my life, I'm keeping a secret from *him*.

Okay, so I kept the fact that I've been in love with him for years a secret too, but that's different. He kept the same secret from me.

With this whole Jesse and Tara thing, I feel like I'm lying to him. There have been so many times I've come so close to telling him. A few nights ago, we were lying in my bed in total darkness, his handsome features illuminated only by the moonlight pouring in through my bedroom window. We weren't talking. We weren't kissing. We were just there, together. It was wonderful and intimate and I thought, in that moment, there was nothing in the world that I couldn't or shouldn't tell him. But still, something held me back.

Here's the thing about Sam. He is so loyal to everyone he loves, but he's especially loyal to his bandmates. If I told him, there's no way he would be able to keep that secret from Cory. He'd feel honor-bound to tell him. Unfortunately, it would also be a huge betrayal, not just to Jesse, but to me, because of course, if I had told him, I would have sworn him to secrecy. He already has so much on his plate, I didn't want to burden him with one more thing to fret about. So I didn't tell him. I haven't told anyone. And I haven't talked to either Jesse or Tara since that day. That won't last long, however, since I know Jesse will be at my birthday celebration a few days after Christmas. It's my twenty-first, so Sam has it in his head that we have to have this huge party and invite everyone we know since we'll actually be at home and not holed up in some hotel room in a random city. That's all fine by me, but I really don't know how I'm going to face Jesse. It's going to be so awkward, especially since Cory will be there too. Maybe as long as Tara doesn't show up, though, everything will be fine.

I hope so, anyway.

Right now, I don't want to think about any of that. I want to concentrate on getting my house ready for movie night. Most of the living room area is clean, but the kitchen is a total wreck. I decided to bake Christmas cookies earlier to surprise everyone. I might not be a professional chef, but I make pretty amazing desserts if I do say so myself. I've stocked our refrigerator with milk and fresh eggnog and I also have a whole box of hot cocoa mix waiting in the pantry.

It won't be the party of the year by any means, but it will be very festive. And I think that's what really counts.

Acknowledgements

As always, I'd like to thank God, my Lord and Savior.

Thank you to my family, my mother and father, for their love and never-ending support. I don't know what I would do without your constant encouragement and belief that your daughters can do anything.

Thank you to my editors, Hannah Alvarez and Kathleen Farmer. I love you both so, so, so much. You are brilliant, amazing women and two of my most trusted friends. I would be totally lost without both of you.

Thank you to my amazing director, Jalitza Delgado! I love you so much and I can't wait to see you and our boys come to life on screen!

Thank you to all musicians who create and inspire. Whether you sing, write, play an instrument, or practice theory, the world as we know it would not be the same without you. Music makes the world a better place, as you well know.

Thank you to all who read, and especially to all of you who have read BOY BAND. Words will never be able to adequately express how important you are to my life and to the lives of authors everywhere. You are so, so loved.

Finally, a huge thank you to my very best friend, my twin soul, and my favorite person in the world, my sister, KJ. If it wasn't for you and the countless hours we spent watching music videos on YouTube, this book would not exist.

© 2017 by Fervent Images – Tim Malek

JACQUELINE E. SMITH is the award-winning author of the CEMETERY TOURS series, the BOY BAND series, and TRASHY ROMANCE NOVEL. A longtime lover of words, stories, and characters, Jacqueline earned her Master's Degree in Humanities from the University of Texas at Dallas in 2012. She lives and writes in Dallas, Texas.

Made in United States
Orlando, FL
01 March 2022

15270609R00124